M000285570

EIGHT WAYS TO TEQUILA

An Althea Rose Novel

TRICIA O'MALLEY

Lovewrite Publishing

EIGHT WAYS TO TEQUILA

An Althea Rose Novel

Copyright © 2021 by Lovewrite Publishing
All Rights Reserved

Editor: Jena O'Connor

All rights reserved. No part of this book may be reproduced in any form
by any means without express permission of the author. This includes
reprints, excerpts, photocopying, recording, or any future means of
reproducing text.

If you would like to do any of the above, please seek permission first by
contacting the author at: info@triciaomalley.com

To Rona & Dave – thank you for your unconditional support, delicious desserts, and serious boogie skills. All my love.

THE WORLD IS FULL OF MAGIC THINGS, PATIENTLY WAITING FOR YOUR SENSES TO GROW SHARPER. – W.B. YEATS

Chapter One

IT WASN'T LIKE I'd meant to send Rafe across the line and through the veil that separated our world from the spirit world. It's just that, well, these things happened with me. On my best days, I'd only spill coffee on my dress. On my worst, well, I'd screw up a magick spell or two.

Some with worse consequences than others.

I wasn't going to point out that it was my tendency to make mistakes in magick that had first gifted Miss Elva, our resident voodoo priestess and magickal goddess, with the annoyance we had come to know and love – well, tolerate – as Rafe. But as I looked at the stubborn set of her jaw, I was convinced that I should hold that little reminder in my back pocket while she worked herself down from a rage.

A silent Miss Elva was a terrifying thing, that's for sure.

"We'll get him back," Luna, my best friend and business partner, stepped between the two of us like a referee ready for a cage match. "We can get him back. He can't have gone all that far."

"We can't do another spirit summoning spell this close to the last one. It's far too dangerous," Miss Elva said. Her hands landed on her waist and I felt my shoulders hunch as I waited for her to berate me.

"We'll figure it out. We always do," Luna promised.

"Or, you know, maybe we live without him for a bit and see if we like it?" I said.

Oops. Miss Elva's eyes widened and she sucked in her breath, sounding like a bull about to charge. Luna turned on me, her mouth rounded in shock.

I'm Althea Rose and today might just be my last day on Earth.

"How can you say that after all he's done for you?" Miss Elva crossed her arms over her chest and tapped her neon trainers on the floor.

"Erm...what exactly has he done for me again?" I skirted the table on my back porch and eased toward the door that went into my house. We'd just dispatched an entire yard full of zombies, and if there was ever a time that called for a drink – it was now.

"Rafe has a mouth that doesn't measure up for what he's packing down there, if you get what I'm saying." Rosita, a madam ghost that had known Rafe when they were both alive, shrugged one shoulder and flitted past me. "He's been nothing but a jerk to Althea. Why should she care?"

"Because I like Rafe and Althea is my friend." Miss Elva said this quietly. Again, a soft-spoken Miss Elva was far more terrifying than a loud one. My stomach instantly twisted in knots.

"You're right, Miss Elva. I don't particularly care for Rafe, but he's grown on me in his own weird way. And I know he means something to you." What that was, I couldn't say, but I held that part back. "I'll do my best to help you get him back. How soon can we do a spell?"

"If you actually care about me, you'll take your damn magick seriously for once. We can't do a spell until the next full moon."

"But...why? You two are powerful enough. Can't you bring him back?" I was decidedly close to whining, I realized, and bit my lip as I guiltily eyed Miss Elva.

"Your magick is attached to both his arrival here and his departure. It's your signature we'll need to pull him back through." Luna gave me a serious look. I knew that look. It meant I was about to be subject to a long talk about responsibility and claiming my magick. How do I know? Well, I'd heard this talk a time or two before. The problem was that we'd been so busy lately that I'd barely had time to help my regular clientele, let alone attend magick university or whatever.

Okay, *maybe* I'd avoided studying up on it as well. I don't know why, really. You'd think I'd be super enthused to know that I carried more power than just my psychic abilities. I think there was a part of me that resisted because I wasn't ready for change. I liked my life as it was. Running the Luna Rose Tarot & Potions shop with Luna made me happy. My fear was, if I added more magick in, then more would be required of me. When, in all reality, sometimes less *was* more. I wanted balance in my life, not more responsibilities. Magick certainly felt like a pretty big responsibility to me. But it didn't look like my life was going to slow down anytime soon, so perhaps not embracing my magick was doing my friends a disservice.

"Miss Elva." I walked over to her and put my hands on her arms, meeting her warm brown eyes. "I promise I will do everything in my power to bring Rafe back."

"I'll hold you to that. I'm so stressed out now! I have to go shopping to calm down." Miss Elva grabbed her tote bag.

"Um, where are you going shopping? Most of the stores are closed." Luna pointed out as she picked up her bag.

"Didn't I tell you my new thing? I follow these Instagram Live shows. My favorites are the vintage jewelry ones. They try all the pieces on and you can bid on them."

"I wasn't aware you were even on Instagram." I arched a brow at Miss Elva in surprise.

"Are you kidding me? I've got fifty thousand followers on Instagram. I post several times a day. I have pre-orders for my Elva line that are pages long. I can't believe you don't follow me." Miss Elva shot me another disapproving look. And here I'd thought we could move on from her low opinion of me…

"I…I don't have an Instagram account," I admitted.

"I swear…" Miss Elva clucked her tongue and shook her head. "It's like…what are you doing with your time all day? You should be building up a social media presence for your business. Studying your magick. Leveling up, Althea. Don't you agree?"

"Um, yes?" I asked. I couldn't bring myself to tell Miss Elva that much of my free time was spent finding new things to season my popcorn with and obsessively reading celebrity gossip magazines.

"That's what I thought. I expect more of you going forward, Althea."

I was left at my front door with a serving full of disapproval and a backyard full of bodies that the coroner's team was doing their best to dispose of. As days went, I'd score it pretty closely with either when I lost my virginity and learned that sex does not automatically come with a side of orgasms or the day that I peed my pants in third grade. It was a toss-up really.

Chapter Two

AFTER DECIDING that the time for personal growth wasn't when a team of government personnel were discretely disposing of dismembered body parts in my backyard, I holed up in my bedroom with Hank, my adorable Boston Terrier, and a two-pound bag of Gardetto's to watch a television show about housewives who had too much time and money on their hands. I woke, groggy, with a pretzel stuck to my cheek and the doorbell ringing downstairs. Hank shot off the bed in a flurry of barks and raced downstairs to defend his territory.

"Shit." I picked the pretzel off my face and briefly contemplated eating it, before shoving myself off the bed and standing up. I pulled a soft robe in a red tie-dye print from where I'd thrown it over my chair and wrapped it around my body before padding slowly downstairs. Hank danced by the front door, letting out intermittent yelps, and glanced over his shoulder at me as though to urge me to hurry up. Pausing at the door, I took a deep breath and reminded myself to only open it a crack. I had learned my lesson after my last foray into being gossip magazine fodder, and I could guarantee that I was not remotely camera ready. If there was a news truck on my doorstep, I would snap that door closed faster than a stripper tucking a dollar in her bra.

But when I saw who was on my doorstep, everything was forgotten as I flew out of the door.

"Mom!"

Abigail Rose, psychic to the stars, posed on my front porch in leather pants, a glittering t-shirt, with a slouchy bag on her shoulder. Her flaming red hair was artfully arranged, her eyes shaded by Chanel, and her lipstick precisely applied. She pursed her lips briefly as she glanced down at my robe.

"Althea."

"I know. Don't judge. I have a doozy of a story for you." I threw my arms around my mom, tears pricking my eyes as her arms came around me and pulled me in for a tight hug where she swayed lightly back and forth like a metronome.

"I've missed you. And, while I was meant to be on my way to the Seychelles, my guides insisted I was needed here. We canceled our trip and turned right around. What's wrong, darling?"

"We?" I asked. Pulling back, I peered around my mother to see my father, Mitchell Rose, pulling luggage from the trunk of a rental car. In a rumpled tie-dye t-shirt from Grateful Dead's '72 tour, loose cargo shorts, and white socks and tennis shoes, he was every aging hippie

I'd ever seen. How my endlessly fashionable mother hadn't managed to steamroll him into dressing differently was still a mystery to me – but I loved him the more for it.

"Dad!"

"Hiya, pudding. Nice robe!" Dad waved to me while he cheerfully lugged bags onto my porch.

Then it hit me. Bags. On *my* porch.

"Are you staying with me?" I asked, trying not to imply that I wasn't enthused about the idea.

"Naturally, honey. You know we don't like that motel downtown. Particularly since the last murder there." My mother sniffed and then bent down to pick up Hank. More points in her favor – Abigail Rose could be wearing thousands of dollars in Chanel and she wouldn't blink an eye at picking up my dog and cuddling him close, like he was her grandson. I couldn't resent someone who didn't give two hoots about dog hair on her fancy clothes. "There's my sweet angel baby. Have you been getting fed enough? He feels skinny to me, Althea."

"He's an active pup," I said. Dad reached me and pulled me into his arms and I inhaled the comforting scent of cinnamon gum and…incense? I'll call it incense. Just in case there were still a few police officers wandering my property.

"You look tired," Dad said.

"I am. Come in, come in. Let's get off the porch." I peered down the street to make sure there weren't any news vans before turning to go back inside. Walking across the living room, I paused at my sliding glass doors to survey the yard. Miraculously, it seemed like the team had done its job and aside from my destroyed tomato plants and trampled grass, there were no other indications of the turmoil from yesterday. Like stray body parts. "Hank has to go outside, Mom."

"Of course, he does. Does my sweet baby need to make potty wotty?" Abigail crooned to Hank as she carried him through the house, leaving her bags to be brought in behind her. Hank licked her face in response and she laughed. "That's a good boy then. Let's take care of your business so we can all sit down with an espresso and have a chat about why your mama looks like she just rode out a hurricane."

"I only have coffee, Mom," I said cheerfully as I opened the door for Hank. Her little hiss of disapproval made me smile as I watched Hank race outside and run around the yard. He had to sniff all the scents and re-mark his territory, and I knew it would take him a while. Walking further outside, I doublechecked that the police had locked my gate and that Hank had a safe area to run around, before I returned to my kitchen and sized up my parents.

"I raised you better than this." My mom turned to me, holding my coffee pot in her hand.

"You've been in Europe too long," I said. "I just make a quick cup of coffee and then I'm out the door."

My mother slid my father a look and he laughed.

"I'll take care of it, love. But, you haven't gotten so high and mighty that you can't enjoy a simple cup of coffee with your daughter right now, have you?"

"No, of course not." My mother looked at him as

though he'd accused her of stealing handbags. "I am perfectly capable of drinking straight coffee."

"Right," I said.

"No frother, I suppose?" Abigail looked hopefully around.

"Black coffee and hazelnut creamer is what I have available for Your Highness this morning." I laughed and took the pot from her hands as she crinkled her nose in disgust at my words. "And you'll pretend you don't like it."

"She loves that creamer. I don't think they even sell it where we last stayed. Don't think I haven't seen you sneak it in your coffee, my love." Dad twinkled at Mom while she simpered at him. It was something I'd always loved about their relationship. Two wildly different people had found a way to live, work, and love together – all while being charmed by each other's differences. My father, a highly regarded music professor, was more often than not amused by my mother, and she was equally as besotted with him. For all intents and purposes, they never should have fit together, and yet they went together like chocolate and peanut butter.

Speaking of…I opened the freezer and poked my head into it wondering if I still had a carton of chocolate peanut butter cup ice cream. Who was I kidding? No ice cream lasted longer than a day or two tops in my house.

"Looking for ice cream? This must be a bad story." Dad came over and threw his arm around my shoulders, pulling me close and pressing a kiss to my head. "It's good to see you, kiddo. It's been too long."

"It really has. I've been meaning to come visit. But

with Hank…and the shop taking off. Well, it's been tricky to get away."

"We should've come back sooner. Your mother got a few high-profile clients that wanted us on call for a while. It was time consuming, but very lucrative."

"Honestly, darling, we could take years off now if we wanted to after those clients. We've cleared our schedule and are here for you." My mother squinted at the coffee pot that began to dribble dark liquid into the pot.

"Years? You're here for years?" My voice went up a note. Hank skidded back inside, having taken care of business, and now with only one thought in mind – breakfast.

"God, no. As much as I love you, darling, I can't live in this little town again. But I know when I'm needed, so here I am."

"What, specifically, do you think you're needed for?" I still leaned into my father, but tilted my head at my mother in question.

"Why, for your magick, of course, darling. It's time to teach you who you are, isn't it? Or am I wrong there? I was certain you finally seemed ready to embrace your other talents." Abigail clapped her hands when the pot finished filling.

"I…I screwed up. Just yesterday. And, actually, several times before this. I didn't think I needed to learn – I'm still not sure. I like my life as it is. I don't want it to change."

"Oh pumpkin." My dad smiled at me, his warm brown eyes kind as he studied me through his glasses. "Don't you know that's the only thing you can count on in this world?"

"You can run...you can hide..." My mom's eyes lit up when I pulled out the hazelnut creamer from the fridge.

"Yeah, yeah I get it. Okay, you're right. The time has come. Teach me your ways, oh wise one."

"I knew it!" My mother clapped again and then did a little twirl in the kitchen, Hank joining her dance. "But, first...coffee."

Chapter Three

IT WASN'T every day that my parents came to visit, and it certainly wasn't every day that I woke up after a zombie apocalypse in my backyard. Grateful that it was the weekend, and I had no clients on my schedule, I settled onto the couch on my back porch with my less-than-perfect cup of coffee and grinned at my parents. They'd automatically curled up next to each other on the other couch, my mother leaning into my father's side, his arm draped loosely around the back of the couch over her shoulders, and a warm feeling of love washed over me. When people you care about are away for so long, it's sometimes hard to remember just how great you feel in their presence. It was like that with my parents. They were some of the best people I knew, and I always missed them when they traveled, however it wasn't until they were back with me that I realized just *how* much I missed them. Being near them was like being cocooned in a wave of love and acceptance.

My mother eyed my ratty bathrobe again and sniffed. Okay, so maybe their love came with just a touch of judgment. I mean, if I was being honest with myself, I probably should buy a new bathrobe. But it had become like a comfort blanket to me. Worn down to the perfect softness, I could wrap myself in it and hide from the outside world all I needed.

Hank raced up from the backyard where he'd continued on his task of marking all the bushes that had been trampled over yesterday. Dropping a ball at my feet, he tilted his head at me and looked up expectantly.

"Of course, buddy." I leaned down and tossed the ball across the yard. In seconds Hank was back, but this time he veered to my father who had snapped his fingers at Hank.

"I miss throwing this ball for him. You need to work on your arm, Althea." My dad heaved the ball across the yard and Hank took off with a delighted yelp, for he hadn't had a good throw to race after since…well…since the last time Trace had been over. Thinking of him, my heart did a funny little shiver in my chest. I really needed to get clear on my self-reflection and just, what exactly, I planned to do with some of the current problems in my life.

"What I lack in distance, I make up for in repetition. Longevity, Dad. You'll tire out soon enough, but I can throw that ball without thinking for hours at a time."

"Well, he's lucky to have you. He seems happy enough. You aren't leaving him at home alone too often, are you?" Abigail skewered me with a look.

"Some days he stays home. But I take him to Lucky's with me or wherever else I'm going. He's welcome most places in town."

"And why shouldn't he be? He's positively a gentleman! So, now that we're settled, why don't you tell us what's been going on? Because my guides were pretty insistent about us coming home to you." Abigail sipped her coffee and gave me a look that seemed to say – whatever you've done wrong I might yell, but then I'll hug you after.

"Oh, goddess, where to begin?" Sighing, I tucked my feet under myself and looked out across the yard. I spoke to my parents fairly often, they were up to date on most things in my life, but I'd shielded them from some stuff – like the number of times I had gotten myself into trouble lately. As in life-threatening trouble. I grimaced, thinking about how to tell them about the scraps I'd gotten myself into. Well, in all fairness, some of these situations had found their way to my doorstep – it wasn't like I was always out there looking for trouble. It just seemed like I was a magnet for it.

"Start with why my spirit guides told me to hustle my beautiful butt back to Tequila Key," Abigail suggested.

"Likely because of the zombies." I sighed and squeezed my nose.

"Actual zombies?" My dad pursed his lips.

"No. A fledgling necromancer. Basically, she was trying to bring her daddy back. But with untested magick, she wreaked a lot of havoc."

"Has she been caught?" Abigail asked.

"She has. And the bodies, from what I can tell," I peered out into the backyard, "have all been cleaned up."

"Is that all? Were you…or are you in any danger?" My mother leveled me with a look.

"I…no. But I have been. Actually, quite a bit in recent months."

"You failed to mention that, Althea Rose," Mitchell said. I hunched my shoulders at my father's tone.

"I didn't want to worry you." Was I whining?

"It's our job to worry. Come on, kiddo. Lay it on us."

So, I did. I told them about all the times I had been in danger in recent months. I filled them in on all the ups and downs with Trace and Cash. I winced when I told them about the fumbling and mishaps with my magick. By the time I'd finished, the coffee cups were empty, and my mother was craning her neck to look toward my liquor cabinet.

"It's too early for alcohol." I smiled at her, knowing what Abigail was about.

"Nonsense. They serve mimosas at breakfast, don't they? Or a bloody Mary."

"Just coffee for you if you're going to teach Althea any of your magick." My father patted my mother's leg companionably.

"That's the part you're focusing on? Not my brushes with death?" I raised an eyebrow at my mother.

"Well, you're not dead. So that's a positive. And I can't go back and change the past. Well, I suppose I could, but I don't like tampering with the past too much. Your love life is your own choice, though I can tell you who I'd like to see you with. So, that leaves your magick. It's time for you to learn about the other gifts that I've passed to you."

"Wait…who do you think I should be with?" I brushed my mother's words about my magick aside. Priorities here, people.

"I think you'll make the right choice for you." Abigail nodded sagely at me. I'm not saying I wanted to punch my mother, but there was a part of me that wouldn't mind pushing her off the couch and sitting on her until she told me what I should do with my love life.

"You're annoying," I said instead.

"I'll say this – listening to your parents about who you should choose for love is not advisable." Mitchell smiled down at Abigail fondly.

"Oh, do you remember how much they hated me?" Abigail laughed.

"They didn't hate you. They just didn't understand you. I mean…if they could love me through eschewing a law degree and touring with the Dead for several years, they could certainly love my choice in a partner. And they came around, didn't they?"

"It certainly took some time."

"Nevertheless…"

"Okay, fine. My magick. I'm shit at it." Sighing, I ran a hand through my curls and tugged. An anxious habit of mine.

"You're not shit at it. You're not shit at anything you put your mind to. You just haven't learned yet." My mother immediately jumped into protection mode. It was one thing I could always count on with my parents. While they could be critical of me at times, they didn't allow anyone else to criticize me – including me.

"I've been too scared to try. Or busy. I'm not sure, exactly. It just feels like I was comfortable staying in my lane, you know? Luna does her magick. I do my readings. And it's a good balance. I wasn't expecting to have to know or explore more abilities. And I guess I'm worried what that will open up for me. I like my life. I don't want to suddenly have to be the person that everyone goes to for a spell or whatever."

"Everything changes, honey. Refusing to learn and grow with your abilities is only going to make things worse for you. You'll block your energy, and it will go stagnant. Your readings will suffer." Abigail uncrossed her legs and stood, coffee cup in hand.

"It sounds to me like you have a boundaries issue, kiddo." My dad smiled gently at me and pushed his glasses back up his nose.

"How so?"

"Just because you can do something doesn't mean you should. Magick isn't like…knowing how to perform a surgery or first aid or something. You have no requirement to perform any spell or ritual for anyone. No matter what. Learning to say *no* is a delightful skill."

"Huh."

"Also, there are ways to manage your time more efficiently so that you can spend time learning your magick," Abigail added. "You already have a long waiting list for your readings. Take another day off per week. Increase your pricing. Guard your time. Make your hours shorter, your prices higher, and I guarantee you'll have even more people clamoring for your services. You'll make more money, have more free time, and your quality of life will be better. Maybe when you were starting out it was good for you to build a reputation, but that is no longer needed. Now, you need to tighten up your business and look at where your time is best spent." My mother, a business guru all of a sudden.

"Luna's swamped, too," I mused. "She's talking about bringing on a helper for her tonics and potions."

"That's an area you could help in as well, if you get better at your magick."

"I really did enjoy helping her with the potions we did last week. It was a really peaceful morning spent in her magicks room. It felt good," I admitted.

"Something to think about," Dad chimed in.

"Come on, Althea. Put more coffee on. We'll need it for what's next." My mom was still standing with her empty coffee cup.

"What's that?" I looked up as a loud knock sounded at my door. Hank exploded into barks and raced to the front of the house. "Oh no. Is it bad? I don't know that I can handle more bad."

"Let's just call it your next learning experience." Abigail beamed at me and I groaned.

"Can't a girl catch a break?"

Chapter Four

I'M NOT SAYING I whimpered before I opened the door, but I might have muffled a small groan. It felt like drama had set up camp on my doorstep and wasn't planning to leave anytime soon.

"Miss Elva! What's wrong?"

Miss Elva stood on my porch in a simple caftan in muted pearl grey tones and an ELVA trucker hat. Her expression was anything but joyful and my stomach knotted as I waited for her to speak.

"My necklace was stolen." Miss Elva swooped inside, her caftan flowing behind her, and I closed the door quickly in her wake. My brain scrambled to make sense of what she'd just said.

"You had a break-in?" I asked. I followed her as she crossed to where my parents stood by the back door.

"Abigail. Mitchell. I'm glad you're here. I can only hope it's to instruct Althea in her magicks?" Miss Elva put her hands on her hips as she studied my mother.

"We can only instruct when she's ready to learn,"

Abigail said. Both women pursed their lips and turned to me with mutually disapproving stares.

"Let's focus on what is important here," I said. I tied the belt of my robe tighter and moved to the kitchen to make another pot of coffee. There was only so much criticism a woman could take first thing in the morning. "You've had a break-in? Were you hurt? Was anything else stolen?"

"I didn't say I had a break-in. I said my necklace was stolen." Miss Elva shook her head at my deductive skills.

"Okay, so you were mugged?" I tried to imagine anyone stupid enough to try and accost Miss Elva on the street. Let's just say I'd put all my money on Miss Elva in a street fight.

"As if." Miss Elva rolled her eyes and accepted the cup of coffee I handed her. I suspected this was going to take a while, so I motioned for her to go outside after I had topped everyone else up.

"Elva, your fashion line is lovely. I've already pre-ordered your tropical print caftan...the one with the flamingos?" My mom smiled at Miss Elva. She was also probably one of the few people in the world who could get away with addressing Miss Elva simply by her first name. I actually felt my heart rate go up when she did, and my eyes darted to Miss Elva to see her response.

"Thank you, Abigail. The pink will look beautiful with your red hair. I don't know why more redheads don't wear that combination. It's stunning."

"Certainly better than yellow." My mother wrinkled her nose at the thought. "I can't pull that off."

"What happened with the necklace?" If we were going

to sit and talk fashion, we could certainly have this conversation later on, couldn't we? Like after I'd had a shower and gotten properly dressed for the day.

"Well, it was just awful! You know those Instagram live jewelry shows I like?" Miss Elva turned to me.

"I mean, you just mentioned them yesterday, so I'm a bit unclear about what they actually are."

"Well, child, they're just too much fun. I follow all these vintage jewelry shops on Instagram, and they have live shows where they try on the pieces and you can bid. They offer discounts and free shipping if you buy on the live show. And you kind of get to know the other regulars who watch the shows, so it's damn fun to chat during the show."

"That does sound fun. Can you recommend a few for me? I do love jewelry." My mother said.

"You can never have enough sparkle. More is more," Miss Elva said. Both women nodded sagely at each other while I rolled my eyes.

"Okay, yes. The show?"

"Well, this was one of my favorite shops – High Square Jewelers. I really like this woman who does the shows, and she was robbed! On the live! It was on camera and everything! And the very necklace I was bidding on was stolen!"

"No way. That's crazy. Where is this shop located?"

"It's in the Keys, so the next town up. Luckily, because those of us watching were able to send help. I watch some shows from around the world and wouldn't have been able to do anything." Miss Elva shook her head sadly. "Now, we have to figure out how to get the necklace back."

"We do? Have you even paid for it yet? I thought you said you just bid on it."

Miss Elva slanted me a glance that had enough warning in it to remind me that I was still on her naughty list for sending Rafe inadvertently over into the veil.

"Of course, we'll do what we can to get you the necklace. Is there a replay? Can we watch what happened?" I asked.

"There is. Here. Look."

We all crowded around Miss Elva's phone and waited while she cued the video up. In moments, a beautiful young woman sat in front of a tray of jewelry and held up a serpentine gold chain necklace with a large purplish stone pendant in a gold filigree setting.

"That's a star sapphire. When the light hits sapphire, a star will shine out from the stone. It's quite powerful, and the flaws of the stone make it more valuable. The thought that the defects can make something better is wonderful. More people need to learn that," Miss Elva said.

"This is a very powerful magickal stone," Abigail commented.

"Now look." Miss Elva ordered, and we all hushed. A shiver of fear worked through me as a cloaked figure snuck into the room and held a gun to the woman's head. The pretty woman holding the necklace froze in place, and I certainly didn't blame her.

"I'll just be taking that." The voice, that of a woman, was somewhat muffled as she leaned over and grabbed the star sapphire necklace from the petrified woman's hands. In a matter of seconds, she'd slipped out the back, leaving the poor woman speechless and gaping at the camera.

"Can you rewind that, Elva? I just want to see something." My mother nibbled her lip as Miss Elva rewound the video and started it again. "There! Can you freeze it. Like two seconds back?"

Miss Elva complied.

"Is there any way to zoom in on that bracelet?" Abigail asked, bending closer to the image on Miss Elva's phone.

"Sure, let me screenshot it and then we can zoom in." Miss Elva did so and then we were able to see the charm bracelet the robber wore in more detail. It was a curb-linked gold bracelet with a single charm hanging from the links. It was an intricately woven star with a little purple stone in the middle.

"Oh great. Those amateurs?" Miss Elva spat out.

"I didn't realize they were still around. What a mess they make of things," Abigail agreed.

"Who? What?"

"That's the symbol for the Seven Star Sister Society." My mother wrinkled her nose as she said it. "They fancy themselves to be witches."

"And they're not?"

"Oh, some of them can be. But the majority of them are largely untrained and meddling with things they don't much understand. I had a time of it twenty years ago cleaning up their messes. Do you remember, Elva?"

"I hate those bitches."

Leave it to Miss Elva to be concise in her feelings. I met my father's eyes, and he just shrugged.

"So…if they aren't all that powerful, can't we just track them down and turn them in?" I asked.

"Depends on how quickly they plan to use that neck-lace," Miss Elva said.

"What are they using the necklace for?" I asked.

"They love star sapphires. Powerful stone, as Abigail pointed out. Because they aren't strong in their own magick, the stone will amplify their spell work. Basically, making a mess of everything. Who knows what they'll try to do with this one?"

"But if they were willing to use deadly force to get this necklace..." Abigail met Miss Elva's eyes.

"Then we've got a problem on our hands."

"So, what's the plan? Can't we just tell Chief Thomas about this?" I asked. Please can we just pass this off to Chief Thomas, I pleaded silently. I'd really rather just take a nap.

"Clear your books for the next couple days." This from my mother while Miss Elva just nodded at me with a determined look on her face.

"Why? Is this necessary?"

"It's time for magicks bootcamp. You've put it off too long. We'll begin training shortly." Abigail rose and looked inside. "First, I'll get refreshed and then order in some food. It's going to be a long weekend."

"I'll run home and get some proper ingredients. Best to call Luna in on this as well." Miss Elva dusted her hands off and sailed out of the house with the same determination she had when she'd strode into it.

"But...but...isn't there something more fun we could do this weekend? It's been ages since I've seen you both." Yes, I was pouting a little.

"Do as your mother says, Althea. You know she'll get

her own way no matter what you say." My father patted my shoulder lightly before disappearing into the house, presumably to bring my mother's luggage upstairs.

"Looks like we'll have guests for a while, Hank."

Hank seemed delighted at the prospect and even though I wasn't looking forward to magick classes, I would be lying if I said I wasn't happy to see my parents.

I guess I was going back to school.

Chapter Five

"I'M A SEA WITCH?" I stared at my mother in disbelief. "I didn't even know that was a thing."

We had moved to Luna's ritual room at her shop, deciding that she'd have the largest inventory of various items needed for rituals. Not to mention, the space was magickally protected and there was plenty of room for the four of us to spread out while they put me through my paces in Witchcraft 101. Although, in all honesty, it felt more like a bootcamp than anything else. It had been a long day of practice, and my hair was in knots with how often I'd run my hands through it in despair, I was covered in soot and burns, and I'd manifested no fewer than four unwanted spirits, which Rosita, our resident ghost madam, had cheerfully helped banish back to their realm. All in all, it had been an exhausting and eye-opening day.

But...I *was* making progress. Luna was pleased with my ability to cast a circle of protection. Miss Elva was happy with how I called the elements and my mother... well, was there ever any pleasing a mother? She'd become less critical as the day had worn on, so I would take that as a win. And then Abigail had the nerve to casually drop this bomb on me like it was nothing.

"Yes, of course." Abigail shrugged as easily as if she was telling me what the weather was going to be like tomorrow.

Luna, seeing an imminent explosion, stepped forward.

"I'm a green witch, Althea," Luna said.

"I thought you were a white witch?" I looked at Luna with confusion.

"I am. But I also have roots in being a green witch. It's why I work so much with herbs and potions. My healing tonics come from the earth. It's all intertwined. The white witch part is my commitment to causing no harm to others."

"So, I'm Medusa?" I asked, reaching up to pat my knotted curls.

"More like Ursula," Miss Elva quipped. I slanted a look at her, and she just laughed.

"I don't know why this is a surprise for you, given your love of the ocean." My mother came to me and wrapped an arm around my shoulder. "Your affinity for all things water-related has shone through. You've always told me how comfortable you feel in the water."

"I do. It feels like a second home for me. But…what does this mean exactly? Like…can I talk to sea creatures and stuff?" I immediately pictured myself commanding an army of sharks to follow my orders.

"Calm down, Ursula. You can't become an ocean over-lord," Miss Elva said. She gave me a look as though she knew exactly what had been going on in my mind and I hunched my shoulders.

"I didn't say I needed to be an overlord," I mumbled. *Need* was a strong word. *Desired* maybe.

"When you work with your magick..." My mother patted my arm and brought my attention back to her. "You'll use rituals and spells that are heightened with the use of water elements as well as the moon cycles. I use more earth elements myself, like grounding and herbal elements. We're all magick, you see. You just need to find your particular brand of it, so to speak, and let it shine. It's not going to look like mine, Miss Elva's, or Luna's. You aren't copying what we're doing here. You're learning the basic rituals and rules of magick, but then it's on you to interpret what that means for you and how your magick manifests. Magick has never been about pushing you into a box, Althea. It's been about giving you the foundation to manifest your power how it best suits you."

I paused, struck by that. Part of my long-held beliefs about magick was that I'd have to follow all the rules exactly or I would constantly be screwing things up. The fear of failure had kept me from learning more, because I didn't know how many more times I would be able to let down Luna or Miss Elva when they needed me in a pinch before I just stopped helping those in need all together. But now, looking into my mother's kind eyes, I realized I'd been fighting the wrong thing. The rules weren't there to hold me back; they were there to set me free.

"You've always been a good student, Althea. You have your father's smarts and his inquisitive nature. There's no reason for you not to at least learn what we can teach you. How you use it from there is up to you," Abigail said.

"At the very least, you'll probably feel more comfortable in difficult situations," Luna said. She'd put a kettle on for water and now the scent of mint filled the room as she poured the boiling water over the leaves. Luna looked casual today in simple skinny jeans and a loose white tank, her hair tucked in a knot at the nape of her neck. I smiled my thanks to her when she handed me a cup of mint tea. Holding it to my face, I let the scent soothe me as I turned the new revelation about my powers around in my head.

"I'm sorry," I finally said. I met Luna and Miss Elva's eyes in turn. They'd borne the brunt of my inexperience more than my mother had. "I should've tried harder – and sooner. I think I had some misconceptions about how learning these things would change me – or change my life. And it's just that…I *like* my life. I want to keep doing what we're doing here. I don't need to constantly have bigger and better and more, more, more. I think I've dug my heels in a bit because I didn't want to lose what I have created for myself here."

"You won't lose it if you don't want to lose it." Miss Elva, in a casual-for-her red caftan with silver and turquoise beading and a trucker hat, shook her head at me. "When you stop learning – or refuse to keep learning – that's more dangerous than change. Because, honey, change is coming whether you like it or not. The more tools you have at your disposal, the better."

"I think I understand that better now. I'm sorry it's taken me so long to get it."

"Hush, child. Don't worry 'bout any of that. We all

have our growth years. Don't ask me about my late twenties. I'd like to block those out, except then I'd forget all those tasty men I sampled." Miss Elva threw her head back and laughed and the tension that knotted my stomach eased.

"Ah, my early twenties for me." My mouth dropped open at my mother's words.

"Mom!"

"Well, honestly, Althea. You can't have thought your father was the only man I've been with?" My mother tilted her head at me in question.

"I can honestly say that I don't think about you with *any* men. Including Dad." Ew, now that thought popped in my head and I wrinkled my nose up. "Okay, we need to change this conversation now."

"I've done some digging on the Seven Star Sisters Society," Luna said smoothly, noting my distress.

"Ah yes, those little pests." Miss Elva took her cup of tea and settled into a seat on the other side of Luna's workshop. My mother tucked in next to me on the loveseat and Luna leaned back against her workbench to look at her notes.

"This particular branch of *witches* is..." Luna looked up from her notes, "and I use that term in the loosest sense possible."

"They're posers," Miss Elva grumbled, and I raised an eyebrow at her.

"Did you just call them posers? I don't think I've heard anyone use that term since..." I trailed off as Miss Elva gave me a warning look. "I mean, it's just been a while."

"I'm trying it out. Everything that is old is new again,

didn't you know? I think I might bring back *bitchin'* as well. Oh, and shoulder pads in t-shirts. That's a thing now. I think it will make my waist look smaller."

We all took a sip of our tea and looked away.

"I'm telling you – shoulder pads are back. Fight it all you want." Miss Elva rolled her eyes.

"Bitchin'!" I said and Miss Elva nodded.

"See? It works for everything."

"The society aligns themselves with all things stars. So, instead of moon elements or earth elements, they believe the power comes from the stars. Because of this, they have taken on the star sapphire stone as their official magickal channeling stone. Which is a bit silly, if you think about it – those stones are quite expensive so every ritual they do they'll have to get new ones or cleanse and recharge the ones they have if the stones aren't destroyed," Luna said, taking back control of the conversation.

"They are just trying to be fancy," Miss Elva said.

"Star sapphires do have some interesting properties. Plus, they're gorgeous. I'd much rather wear one than use it in a ritual though," Abigail said.

"So would I. Except they stole mine." Miss Elva glowered into her cup.

"Rude," I agreed.

"Here's the disconcerting bit. I've learned they might be trying to do a glamor goddess ritual," Luna said.

"Oh, for f…" Miss Elva bit down on the rest of what she was about to say.

"What's a glamor goddess ritual? Is it what you do to keep your clothes from getting stains?" I narrowed my eyes at Luna.

"They're trying to raise a goddess. In doing so, they hope to have her beauty and glamor powers bestowed upon them," Luna continued.

"Didn't answer my question," I muttered into my teacup. Luna smoothly ignored me.

"Can't they just get Botox and stop messing with realms they don't understand?" Miss Elva griped.

"That would be ideal, yes. But it seems like they are going to do what they want."

"And we need to stop them?" I looked up at the silence and was met with three glowering stares. "What? I was just asking. I mean…technically speaking, what's the harm in letting them mess around with magick and screw things up for themselves? What does that have to do with us?"

"My necklace, Althea?" Miss Elva crossed her arms over her chest.

"Oh, right. The necklace. Maybe…"

"Don't even say that I need to pick another necklace. I've been looking for years for the perfect star sapphire necklace. That one is mine. It called out to me. It begged me to take it home. Now we have to go rescue my baby. Not to mention that these amateurs will probably explode the Tequila Key if they mess with this kind of magick."

"So. We just need to figure out when their next ritual will be and stop them," Luna said with a small smile.

"It looks like the Orion's belt will be fully above us this week," Abigail said, looking up from her phone.

"What does that have to do with anything?" I asked.

"Orion's belt holds the Three Sisters. The Star Sisters view it as a powerful sign for them," Luna said.

"But can't you see Orion's Belt for a while? Like it

won't just be over us for one night. So how do you know what night this will happen?" I asked.

"Usually when the coordinates put the constellation directly above the ritual spot. They believe the position makes it possible for them to pull the power at its strongest from the Three Sisters." Luna smiled gently at me.

"Bitchin'," I mumbled.

Chapter Six

"YOU'RE certain they're meeting today?"

Miss Elva and I had been designated the task of paying a visit to a few members of the Star Society that Rosita, Miss Elva's ghost, had easily tracked down for us. I'd met Miss Elva at her house for a run-down of what our plan was, and we were currently drinking a delicious mango spiced lemonade on her porch while the sun dipped low in the sky.

"They meet in the café every Tuesday after Bingo. They say it's their book club, but they pour rum into their coffee from flasks and the shop looks the other way." Miss Elva pursed her lips and shook her head. "I can't believe Edna Lewis is part of the Star Society. I always thought there was something odd about her, but just thought it came down to her obsession with collecting Victorian mourning hair jewelry and the number of cats she has."

"Mourning hair jewelry? Is that really a thing still?" I cringed at the thought of wearing someone else's dead hair against my skin.

"Not much anymore. But people collect the old stuff. There's a huge following for it."

"Isn't that…" I shook my head at Miss Elva in confusion. "Just weird? Like you're going to collect jewelry made from the hair of people who died a hundred years ago and wear it now? Like what if the person was a bad person? Now you're wearing their hair around like it's no big deal?"

"You *know* I wouldn't mess with that stuff. Not when so much of my magick requires a personal touch like a lock of hair or a piece of clothing. There's big magick attached to those personal effects. No sir, you will not find me sporting that. Plus, it's just too drab for me. I like sparkles." Miss Elva nodded at me, and it was hard to argue with her, considering today she was wearing a sequin turquoise caftan that made her look like a land-locked mermaid.

"Maybe I need to start watching your jewelry shows. I could do with some more sparkle." I glanced down at my simple black maxi dress where I'd hung a long turquoise and moonstone pendant for a small pop of color.

"That necklace is real pretty, Althea. I know I give you a hard time about your fashion choices, but I think it's just because I want more from you. It's like you're putting in the minimum amount of effort. You don't have the worst eye either, it's just…rumpled."

"My eye is rumpled?" I raised an eyebrow at her.

"Your fashion eye. It's like…you find pretty stuff but then leave it in a ball in your laundry basket and throw it on with the first necklace you grab before you go out the door. Now, maybe you picked the right piece of clothing, but if you'd taken an extra ten minutes and layered a few more necklaces or found a cute sandal, you'd look ten times more presentable."

"But don't you think that's society's programming of us? Having to look a certain way to be fashionable or presentable? Isn't that the patriarchy forcing those ideas on us?"

Miss Elva snorted and muttered something under her breath before giving me that look – the one that said I was about to be treated to another lecture.

"I'm not saying you have to look or dress a certain way. I would think by now you would know that I don't follow trends and like to bang my own drum."

Considering she was currently wearing a caftan covered in a bright turquoise sequins, I could agree with her statement.

"But what I am saying…" Miss Elva continued, "is that it's how you present yourself. If you want to wear neon green leopard print tights with a brown corduroy skirt and a fuzzy grandma sweater – go for it. Fashion should be about what it means to you. However, it *is* about looking like you care about what you put on your body and how you present yourself to the world. If you want to wear pajamas all day and be comfy – that's fine – but then make them fun or interesting to wear. People seem to forget that our clothes, our fashion, our jewelry – well, that's our war paint. That's not just a uniform, but our armor. You can be a warrior princess in pajamas just as easily as you can in a caftan – but show you care. Show your choices are deliberate. You make it seem as though dressing yourself is an afterthought, and unfortunately, people do judge a book by its cover. What you wear, how you carry yourself, and how you look is the first thing people will judge you on before you ever speak a single word. I'm not saying that you can't wear your maxi dresses. I'm saying make it intentional, like you've taken joy in your choices. Whatever those choices are for you."

Here I'd thought I'd come to meet with Miss Elva about catching a robber, but instead I was being served up with more lessons on personal growth. However, Miss Elva was an impassioned orator, and she certainly had a point. If I was going to put the time into stepping into my power, I could also extend that to how I presented myself to the world. And a sea witch wouldn't just wear anything, now would she?

"What do you have in your upcoming line that is perfect for a sea witch?"

"I've got just the dress for you. I made it with you in mind but was waiting for you to ask. In fact, I had the samples delivered last week. I'll get it for you."

"I doubt I'd fit into a sample size…" I trailed off when Miss Elva turned from where she'd walked to her front door and glared at me.

"As if I would make a sample size zero for my collection?"

"Right, right. Got it." I bit back a smile as I heard Miss Elva muttering about my foolish ways from inside her front room before she returned to the porch.

"Here. Now, child, don't say no right away. I made this thinking about you."

I couldn't believe the dress she was holding. It was… well, quite simply, it was stunning. The dress was a silky blue wrap style with shimmering shades of turquoise that blended all the way down to the darkest blue like the deepest depths of the ocean. It was like standing on the deck of a boat and looking down into the water with myriad shades of blue competing with each other. The hemline sparkled with subtle iridescent beading, and the waistline held an intricate tie belt with turquoise and green sequins.

"This…this is how you see me?" My voice caught as I reached out to touch the silky print.

"Of course. I just hope you can see yourself this way, too."

"Oh." Tears pricked my eyes and I laughed, dashing the back of my palm across my cheeks. "I'm sorry. I don't mean to cry. Miss Elva…this is breathtaking. I can't believe you made this for me."

"It should be in your size. I'll send it home with you. We don't have time to try it on now, what with needing to go after Edna and all. But you'll take it home and you'll wear it for me at the right time."

"But…I can't accept this. Don't you want to see it on?"

"I know how it'll look on you, child, 'sho I do. It's you who needs to see."

"Can I just say?" I looked up at Miss Elva with a smile. "I am so proud of you. Your clothing line is going to be incredible."

"Of course it is, honey. Don't you think I know that I'm amazing? I bet you did know that. Because that's how I show up in the world. Now it's your turn." But Miss Elva reached out and squeezed my arm, letting me know she appreciated my words.

"Channel my inner Miss Elva. Got it."

"Or your Ursula."

"Would you knock it off? Can't I be Ariel?"

"Why – so you don't have a voice? You're not waiting for a prince to rescue you, Althea. The only person who can rescue you *is* you."

"Hmpf. Well. Now. The life lessons seem to be abundant this week." I stood and accepted the bag that Miss Elva had tucked the dress into.

"Better get yourself an umbrella, honey. When it rains…it pours."

"We'd better get going," I said and waited as Miss Elva locked up before we walked down her porch steps to my car. I tucked the dress carefully in the back seat and then got behind the wheel. Once Miss Elva was in, I looked over at her. "What's the plan exactly?"

"Well, I've been thinking on this. We can't just barge into the coffee shop and jump them. But I know Edna's the leader. She's the oldest one now and, despite her obsession with hair jewelry, she's quite vain. This glamour thing sounds right up her alley. I think I'll just wait and have a little chat with her in the parking lot."

A little chat from Miss Elva in a parking lot sounded like a terrifying thing. I immediately hissed in a breath at the thought.

"Is…this little chat of yours involving magick?"

"It shouldn't. Not unless Edna tries something. I want to see if I can figure out where they're doing their rituals. She'll give herself away, I'm sure of it. She won't have the necklace on her tonight. They'll be charging it in the starlight somewhere and getting it prepped for the ritual.

Right now, this is more of a warning. I want her distracted. I want her worried. And I want her running scared."

I gripped the wheel more tightly at Miss Elva's tone.

"Have you been watching your crime shows again? You sound like you're about to confront a rival gang member."

"She might as well be. She's not a friend to the magickal community. These sisters cause a lot of problems and rarely do anything helpful."

"But if they can't really do much magick, just how many problems are they actually creating?" I turned the car down the main drag of Tequila Key which was nothing more than a few blocks of shops and restaurants fighting for prime real estate with water views. At this time of night, kids careened by clutching ice cream cones in their hands and couples walked hand-in-hand on their way to dinner. The sun was just setting, and it cast a shimmer of pink light onto the clouds above. Somewhere, a reggae beat pulsed, and the cry of a seagull circling overhead reached me through my open window.

"Well, child, let's just have a look at all the ways your improper use of magick has created problems." Miss Elva shot me a look and my neck tightened. "You brought Rafe through. You brought Rosita through…"

"Okay, okay, okay…that's enough. I got it." The list was a long one and I didn't need Miss Elva cataloging all the ways I'd failed this year. "Let's go back to me being a powerful sea witch in a gorgeous dress. I much preferred that conversation."

"Wouldn't we all? All I'm saying is that these sisters cause problems. They've been quiet for a bit – or at the very least I haven't had to clean up any of their messes in a while. But now they've really pissed me off. Stealing my necklace? For a stupid glamor spell? No, child, that's just not happening. 'Sho isn't.'"

"Right. Got it." I was lucky enough to spy a parking spot around the corner from the little coffee shop where the sister society was apparently indulging in their spiked coffees after their bingo game. Pulling the car into the space, I turned it off and looked over at Miss Elva. "Now what?"

"Now we wait."

"You're going to just wait and jump out at her?"

"Damn straight. Bitch won't see what's coming."

"Again, might I stress that you are not in a gang?" I asked, widening my eyes at her. "We're just here to gather information."

"I'll gather information, honey. Don't you worry."

"I'm beginning to get worried."

"We just have different ways of extracting information is all." Miss Elva's eyes gleamed in the light from the streetlamp, and I leaned over and banged my head lightly on the steering wheel.

Somehow, I didn't think this was going to be a simple conversation.

Chapter Seven

"GO! GO! GO!"

I started as Miss Elva launched forward and then caught herself against her seatbelt, struggled for a moment, and then all but tumbled from the car to block the path of a woman who had come out of the coffee shop and down the side lane. The woman looked shocked as Miss Elva righted herself – so would I if a flurry of silk and sequins bounced out of a car and landed at my feet. Gingerly, I slipped from my seat and rounded the hood to stand next to Miss Elva.

"Elva," the woman said, her lip curling in disgust as she sized up Miss Elva. My eyebrows shot clear to my hairline and I waited for Miss Elva to pulverize her.

"Edna." Miss Elva glared right back.

I glanced around as the silence strung out and waited for some tumbleweed to blow down the street. The women looked like they were meeting at high noon in an old Western movie. Edna was not what I had been expecting from Miss Elva's depiction of her. I had imagined an aging crone wearing a frumpy sweater. Instead,

Edna was tall and slender, her salt-and-pepper hair slicked tightly back in a severe bun, and her makeup applied tastefully. She wore white palazzo pants with a striped boatneck shell, and a twist of gold gleamed at her throat. I immediately spotted the simple gold bracelet with the charm on it, a twin to the one in the video, and my chin went up.

"Nice bracelet," I said.

Edna's gaze turned to me and her blue eyes skewered mine before she gave me a quick glance and sniffed.

"It's a silly charm bracelet my mother gave to me. They make them in the tourist shops in Miami. I keep it for sentimental purposes. But they're a dime a dozen, really."

"That's a lot of information about your bracelet, Edna. Is there a reason you feel the need to explain so much?" Miss Elva said, hands on hips.

"Merely being polite, Elva. A trait which you struggle with, seeing as you haven't even introduced me to your…friend."

"My name is Althea Rose. And you are?" I cut in before Miss Elva tackled the woman right on the street. The tension bouncing between these two clearly spoke of years of hate.

"Ah, Abigail Rose's wayward daughter. Yes, I've heard of you. And how is that cozy little business of yours?"

Ohhhh-kay I was starting to see where Miss Elva's hatred stemmed from.

"Booming. And hardly wayward, seeing as I settled in the same town I grew up in," I said, pasting a cheerful smile on my face. "And I didn't catch your name?"

"Edna Lewis."

"And what is it you do, Edna?" I smiled, pleasant as could be.

"She's a seamstress," Miss Elva said.

"I run a couture boutique specializing in custom evening and wedding gowns," Edna supplied smoothly.

"Seamstress," Miss Elva whispered. I saw a flicker of rage behind Edna's sharp blue eyes.

"That sounds lovely, I'm sure. Though there can't be much demand for couture in our little town." There. I'd made a little dig at her shop, just because she'd been rude about mine. Feeling better, I met her eyes.

"Well, not with the set you spend your time with," Edna said, her gaze flicking over me again.

Damn it. Maybe we *should* take this woman down.

"And aren't I grateful for that?" I mused.

"Is there something you need, Elva?" Edna shifted her gaze, cutting me out, and I really just wanted to reach over and mess up her hair or something. Her composure deeply annoyed me.

"Funny you should mention it – there is."

"I don't have much time. So, if you can get on with it then?" Edna hoisted her purse higher on her shoulder and tapped her foot on the ground.

"Have you been watching the astrological reports for this upcoming week?" Miss Elva asked.

"Why on earth would I do that?" Again, a flicker of something behind Edna's ice-cold eyes.

"Oh, I'm sure just for fun. Don't we all like taking a look at the moon? And the stars?"

"Honestly, Elva. You've always been just a step away from being committed, but you might have finally taken the leap into insanity. I really don't have the time to stand here and listen to you babbling about the moon."

"And the stars," I piped in.

"Whatever it may be. What is it you need to know?" Edna sighed and glanced around.

"Orion's Belt looks like it will be above us this week."

"Lovely. Why don't you go tell someone who cares?" But this time, a ripple of unease passed over Edna's face.

"I think you do care. You care very much, don't you, old girl?" Miss Elva swaggered a step forward and I looked to the sky and took a deep breath. She'd gone from gang member to cowboy. We needed to work on her approach.

"Who are you calling old, you vapid twit?" Edna countered, her mask dropping. Ah, so maybe Luna had been right about the star society wanting to raise a glamor goddess.

"I call it like I see it. Seems to me you're messing with something you don't much know about. Again. And again. When will you learn, Edna?" Miss Elva asked.

"I find it hard to believe that you have any actual idea what you are talking about. Here you are, insulting me on the street and talking nonsense about constellations. You've finally gone and lost your mind, Elva. It doesn't surprise me. You've never been all there anyway."

"I'm saner than I've ever been, actually, Edna. Not only do I look fabulous, but I have a fashion line that is about to explode while you're messing with things you don't understand in the hopes of becoming ageless. It doesn't work that way, honey. You can't fight time. I mean, *I'm* doing a good job of it. But you're a lost cause."

Miss Elva pointed to her admittedly flawless skin and I thought Edna was about to pop. Gingerly, I rocked back on my heels and waited for her response.

"I suppose we have different definitions of fabulous."

Man, she was good, I thought with a grimace.

"There's only one definition, honey. And when you look it up in the dictionary, you'll see my picture blowing you a kiss."

Right, so now Miss Elva had resorted to school-girl insults. This was going nowhere, and I really had no idea what she was going to accomplish.

"You're exhausting, as always, Elva. I need to get home."

"Still living above that little shop of yours? Or did the landlord boot you for not making rent?" Miss Elva smiled.

"I bought a beautiful home out on Coral Ridge lane, actually. It's custom-built with only the best finishes. You wouldn't know anything about that with your rickety little shack you live in on the wrong side of town."

"Is that right? I didn't know that there was a wrong side of town in Tequila Key."

"Well, unless you talk to Theodore," I added. Theodore Whittier, Mayor of Tequila Key, was determined to keep the upper-class citizens on one side of the town and away from us miscreants. His plan wasn't going well, but a few people had bought into his overpriced housing development. The problem was – he'd picked the wrong town for those kinds of sentiments. Tequila Key liked being quirky, and generally speaking most people enjoyed the blend of personalities found here.

Both women ignored me.

"You're just jealous because I have a water view," Miss Elva said.

"So do I." Edna hissed back.

Seriously, what was the point of this?

"At least I have a private back yard."

"As do I. A manicured and private one. Surrounded by lovely old growth trees with a perfect view of the night sky."

"Oh, is that right? I thought you didn't care about constellations," Miss Elva smiled.

"It has nothing to do with constellations and everything to do with having a nicer view. You've always been an infuriating woman. Honestly, I have no time for your nonsense." Edna made a move to push past Miss Elva.

"Pick up any new jewelry lately, Edna?"

"Excuse me?" Edna paused, her eyes on Miss Elva, and I swear I could have reached out and felt the tension that strung like barbed wire between them.

"Just a question. Since you're so into fashion and all."

"I'm sick of your questions, Elva. Get out of my way, you heifer. You're a menace to this town is what you are."

Uh-oh. I had thought for a moment that we'd get away from this conversation unscathed. I took a step back as Miss Elva's eyes widened.

"Who are you calling fat… you sickly ostrich?" Miss Elva stepped forward and I reached out to grab her arm. I was shocked when she wrenched her arm away.

"You may think your skin is fabulous, but you'll fall over from a heart attack with all that weight you're carrying. And not soon enough as far as I am concerned. Good riddance." And with that, Edna spat at Miss Elva's feet.

Well. She tried to. But Miss Elva had already stepped forward and it landed on her caftan. The world stilled as Miss Elva looked down at the drippy glob of spit on her pretty caftan.

"I'm a full-figured woman. I'm strong. I'm healthy. And I will outlive you if it's the very last thing I do." Miss Elva's tone had gone scarily low. "You'll spend your life worrying about your looks and berating others while I'll fill mine with lovers, good friends, and joy from pursuing my dreams. But you...if messing with magick and time doesn't screw you over, bitterness will."

"Magick? See? I knew you were cuckoo." Edna shot me a look and then marched past Miss Elva and down the street toward her car.

"Get in the car. Now," Miss Elva ordered me.

"What? What did you do? Why?"

"Now."

I ran around the car and hopped behind the wheel as Miss Elva threw herself in the front seat.

"Drive. Drive. Drive!"

Glancing in the mirror, I pulled out of the parking spot and hit the accelerator. We raced past Edna as she turned, hatred on her face, and grabbed the back of her pants. She scurried toward her car, clutching her butt, while yelling something indecipherable. I darted the car quickly to the left, barely looking for traffic, and glanced in my rearview mirror to see a tree branch snap from a tree and land in the street where my car had been.

"What the hell was that?" I screeched.

"Just pushing some buttons," Miss Elva laughed.

"Did you do something to her?"

"I absolutely did. It took me a while too because I had to try and remember that spell while I was baiting her. I just gave her a bit of an upset stomach. The trots, if you will. All in all, that went perfectly."

"How in the world can you say that went perfectly? If anything, you basically hit a bee's nest with a baseball bat."

"Don't fuss over her. Her power is nothing."

"I just saw her shoot a tree branch in my rearview mirror!"

"Is that right? Hmpf. Maybe she's leveled up. Either way…at least we have her address now."

"Is that what you were looking for? Have you heard of Google, Miss Elva?" I schooled my breath to bring my heart rate down.

"Oh, right. I suppose that would have been easier. But certainly not as much fun."

"We need to work on your idea of fun…"

Chapter Eight

"TOMORROW NIGHT?"

I had hoped for a little more time before this next confrontation, however, it seemed like I wouldn't get it. I'd come into the shop well before opening hours this morning to work on a few of the spells and rituals that the women had been teaching me. I wanted the alone time to practice without eyes on me, and I had been pleased to complete each task with minor issues. Luna had been surprised but happy to find me in her back room when she'd arrived for the day.

"Based on the coordinates of Edna's home, Orion's Belt will be directly over her house tomorrow. It won't move much over the next few days, but if we want it to be exact, then it's likely tomorrow."

"And I'm assuming we have no plan for stopping this ritual?" I groused as I closed my notebook. Luna had already moved to her worktable and had pulled out jars for her elixirs.

"I mean…since we don't know what spells they'll be using we can only do what we always do."

"Screw it up and clean up the mess after?" I teased.

"Maybe not this time." Luna laughed and pulled out her big silver mixing bowl. "The issue is that when you are working with other magickal elements, you won't know everything they've added to the mix. We could do everything perfectly and things could still not end up going well. It's just…well, it's the nature of the beast, I guess. In this instance, it's like watching toddlers chug espresso and then trying to get them down for a nap on time. We may do everything right, but the outcome is still not going to be what we hope for."

"So, how does one plan for that exactly?" I leaned my hip against her table and studied the ingredients she pulled out.

"You learn your own magick the best that you can. And then you use it to diffuse the situation. There's no black and white answer really."

"I can help you with your orders this morning, if you need me to?" I nodded to where she was checking a computer print-out. "My first client cancelled, so I have a little time."

"Are you sure? It would definitely make a difference."

"Yeah, no problem. I enjoyed helping you before. You know…" I picked up the two bottles that Luna pointed to and then leaned over to look at her neatly written instructions. "My mother suggested an idea for me to change up my business a bit."

"In what way?" Luna began to measure and mix her ingredients. She'd already magicked this batch of ingredients with her own bit of power, and the rest was just a careful blend of following her private recipes.

"She thinks that I should only take clients a few days a week. If I cut my hours and bump up my prices, I'll make the same amount of money but also have more time – like to help you with your orders one day a week or something like that. If you need the help."

"Oh my goddess, I *so* need the help. I have been putting off hiring someone because I like the coziness of just the two of us in the shop. It's nice, you know? And it's our sacred space. If you'd be willing to do that – I won't turn down the offer. I'll pay you fairly, of course."

"Good, because I'm expensive."

Luna laughed and then we began to focus on our work, with light Celtic music playing in the background as we bottled creams and elixirs. I told her about the night before and she shook her head at Miss Elva's antics. A tingling at my neck alerted me to a vision, and I closed my eyes, leaning into the table for a moment.

"What's a sprite?" I asked Luna.

"No! Where?" I blinked my eyes open as the bottle Luna was holding clattered to the table and she raced across the room.

"Wait! Where are you going? What *are* you doing?"

"Did you see one?"

"Well, if I don't know what they are, how could I have seen one?"

"Why did you just ask me that?" Luna paused, her hand on the cover of a leather book with an intricate Celtic knot on the front.

"I had a vision. Well, just a brief one. And it was of

something called a sprite and he was wreaking havoc. He seemed pretty cheerful."

"Nasty little buggers. They love chaos. Thrive on it, really. Tricky to get rid of because you have to catch them. Please tell me this vision was not based in Tequila Key." Luna's pretty face had clouded with worry as she looked at me.

"Um." I didn't want to lie to her.

"Okay. Right. We'll need to pivot a bit here. I need to get Abigail on the phone now. We have some prep work to do."

"But…" A knock at the front door had us turning.

"Shit, I'm past opening time. Can you unlock for me? I have to get the till in. And your next client is probably here."

"Not for another fifteen minutes." I checked the slim watch at my wrist and moved through the shop, flicking on the overhead track lights as I did. Luna's side of the Luna Rose Tarot & Potions shop was all elegance and femininity – like walking into a luxe spa. Done up in white and gold, with pretty baskets of crystals and tonics, it oozed class. Whereas my side of the shop, tucked discretely away through a side door, was like going to the circus. Both elements worked for us, but I loved coming over to Luna's side and luxuriating in all the pretty things.

I unlocked the door and pulled it open, grimacing when I saw who it was.

"We're closed."

"Unlikely… as it says you're open." Edna Lewis raised a carefully lined eyebrow at me. Her hair was pulled back in the same severe bun, and today she wore crisp tweed slacks and a shell pink blouse. Demure gold hoops winked at her ears.

"Change in plans. It's the beauty of owning your own business." I stood my ground but then groaned as my client pulled up and honked her horn at me.

"Althea, I'll just be five minutes late for my appointment. I'm on the phone with my kid's teacher." My client, Shelly, a harried mother, shouted from her front window.

"You must have forgotten to cancel your appointment then. Seeing as how you're closed?" Another raised eyebrow and a haughty sniff.

"You can let her in, Althea," Luna said quietly from behind me, and I stepped back, glaring at Edna.

"Touch anything and I don't need magick to lay you out. Understood?"

"My, my. So uncouth." Edna's lip curled in disgust as she stepped in, but even she couldn't hold her disdain as she looked around Luna's shop. "Well, I see at least one part of this has been managed professionally."

"Was that a compliment? And here I thought you weren't able to do those?"

"I'm Luna and a proud owner of this shop. May I help you with something today? Perhaps a skin cream or an elixir to soothe troubled stomachs?"

Have I mentioned how much I love Luna? It took everything in my power not to laugh directly in Edna's face as she pressed her lips together tightly.

"I thought I sensed uselessness."

I looked up as my mother all but floated through the doorway, looking effortlessly cool in faded gold metallic jeans, a white t-shirt with a band name I didn't recognize on it, and a boucle Chanel jacket tossed lightly over her shoulders.

"That must be coming from your daughter," Edna said, whirling to snarl at Abigail.

"Careful, Edna, or it will be more than soiled pants you'll be dealing with." My mother's voice had gone icy and even I felt the chill of it as I stepped back from Edna.

"Mom, I didn't know you were coming by today. I see you know Edna. She was just leaving, wasn't she?"

"I'll leave when I feel like it. But there's nothing for me in this shop anyway." Edna sniffed and looked around. I saw her eyes linger on the eye cream for a moment.

"Are you sure? I have just the thing for those anger lines in your forehead." Luna smiled and used her customer service voice.

"The lot of you are just vile people. I couldn't possibly need or want anything you have to offer. However, I thought I'd come by and serve you a warning."

"A warning? Are you like the magickal police or something? Or is this like in soccer? First a yellow card and next a red card and we're out of the game?" I was really enjoying myself, I realized. There was something somewhat freeing about being openly rude to nasty people. I don't recommend it, as I am sure it would lead to a fight at some point, but damn, it was kind of fun.

"I know what you're up to. And I'm warning you to back off," Edna said, ignoring me, but giving my mother a look.

"I would think it's you who is the one who needs to back off, Edna." Abigail sighed and tapped a perfectly manicured finger against her mouth. "I have to ask you – aren't you tired of this yet?"

"Tired of what?"

"Playing at magick. It never gets you anywhere. When are you going to learn that some things shouldn't be tampered with? How many times have we had to get you out of messy situations that you've caused through your own greed?"

"It's not greedy to try to manifest my powers," Edna sneered.

"It is when your motives aren't pure," Luna said, her tone gentle.

"What would you know? You don't even know me."

"I know of you and your exploits. It sounds like the Seven Star Sisters are looking for immortality. The holy grail. All the money. All the fame. All the glory. That sounds greedy to me, don't you agree, Althea?" Luna said.

"It sure does, Luna."

"You two are peons. You know nothing."

"You'd be silly to underestimate the both of them." Abigail studied her nails. "The two of them hold more power together than your entire little society. Now, I'll be the one to issue you a warning. Return the necklace and stop your ritual attempt or I'll turn you in to the police."

"I have no idea what you are talking about." Edna clutched her purse more tightly to her shoulder. "But I don't take well to threats."

"Edna, I'm going to be straight with you. Stop with this useless ritual. It will get you nowhere. Your power is just not up to it. And that's okay. You have so many other strengths. Go pour this energy into your business. Your hobbies. Your passion. Go live your life in amazing and wonderful ways. Following this…wild goose chase will only lead to despair on your part. It's time to let it go. Move on." Abigail spoke directly to Edna, woman to woman, and even I was moved by her speech.

"I've gained a lot more power than you realize, Abigail. I suggest you watch out for me – because you have no idea who you are dealing with." The lights flicked off above us and a basket of crystals flipped to the floor as Edna pushed past my mother and stormed to her car.

"That was rude!" I called after her.

"Leave it, Althea. She came here to intimidate but ended up giving us more information."

"Like what? That's she an uptight b…" I let my words trail off as my client stepped to the doorway.

"Sorry about that, Althea. The kids are driving me crazy these days!"

"No problem, Shelly. Why don't you come on back with me and we'll get started?" I smiled brightly at Shelly and guided her to my side door to let her through. I glanced back to see Luna and my mother in a heated whispered discussion.

"Don't forget to tell her about the sprite!" I hissed across the room.

"Oh, I don't drink soda anymore, but thanks," Shelly called, and I rolled my eyes before heading into my shop. Clearing my mind, I took a deep breath and smiled at where Shelly sat at my table.

"It's so lovely to see you again. It's been at least a year now, right?"

Chapter Nine

AFTER A NO-SHOW with my last client of the day, I left early, wanting to take a moment to myself to think about a few things. Having both a cancellation and a no-show appointment in the same day was causing me to seriously consider my mother's advice about how to change up my business – and the first step would need to be to secure deposits from clients ahead of time to reserve their appointment. However, in this instance, I was happy for the extra hour at the end of my day as I needed it to think. So, I went where I always went when I needed to recharge – to the water.

My parents were out when I got home. Locking my beach cruiser bike to the front porch, I went inside and greeted a happy Hank. Slipping off my sandals, I grabbed a can of bubbly water, a toy for Hank, and unlocked my back door. One of my favorite things about my backyard, when it wasn't overrun by zombies that is, was the little slice of waterfront that I'd been able to find. Beachfront access was highly prized in the Keys and my little spot had almost seemed to slip through the cracks when I'd found it. I'd put a big fence up around my yard, paid an exorbitant amount to bring sand in and create a man-made beach that Hank could play on, and created a little oasis for myself. It wasn't a large spot, I could maybe fit a few lounge chairs at most, but it was mine and that was all that mattered.

Hank, happy to see we were going to play by the water, did a funny little dance where he dug his paws into the sand, then buried his nose in it and snuffled around. Pulling his head up, he sneezed and then raced around the yard in a fit of zoomies. I launched his stuffed football to him, and he caught it mid-air, before bounding back to me.

Lowering myself onto a lounge chair, I took a moment to just watch the water and breathe. The last few weeks had been full-on, what with one crisis or another and this was the first moment I'd really had with nobody requiring anything of me or talking to me. The water lapped gently at the beach, and a frigate looped lazily in the air high out over the water. I felt myself still, the anxiety that rippled through me loosen, and I smiled as I let the presence of the water recharge me.

A sea witch, I thought. *I'm* a sea witch.

Getting up, I walked gently into the ocean until the water reached my ankles. Instantly, a coolness washed through me, and I realized for the first time that this rush of joy wasn't just the natural energy that water could bring to me. This feeling *was* my power. Connecting with the water was like plugging myself into an electrical outlet. I felt alive, energized, and completely in control. In some areas of my life, it felt like I was a bull in a china shop, but here? The water was my happy place.

Testing it a bit, I brought up Luna's instructions on gentle spell casting. Well, intention-setting, I guess. See? I was screwing up what she would call it and yet I knew what I wanted to do. As frustration wound through me, I paused as my mother's words flashed through my mind.

Your magick doesn't box you in.

Right. Got it. So, whatever Luna called it was her thing. But I was just going to try my thing and see if I could do it and we'd go from there. Glancing around to make sure I was still alone, and that Hank was happily gnawing on his football, I focused on the water that rolled gently across the sand. Focusing, I did a little shove with my mind, wanting to stop the waves from rippling in. At first, nothing happened. But that was okay – I was feeling this out for myself. Again, I whispered my intentions and called to my element of water to listen to me. This time, when I pushed back at the wave rolling in...it paused and reversed directions.

"No way!" I said. Excitement ran through me as my power coursed gently in my veins. It felt like I'd tapped into some universal energy source or something and I began to understand how this power could be addicting for some people. It was intoxicating to control the flow of the natural world. However, I quickly remembered Luna's cautions about disrupting nature too much and released my hold on the water, letting it flow uninhibited back to the beach.

"Hey, kiddo! Whatcha doing?"

I turned and smiled at my dad, who ambled across the yard, a different tie-dye t-shirt on and a beer from a local brewery in his hand. Hank dogged his heels, football in mouth, and happiness flooded me at his nearness.

"It appears I'm learning magick."

"That's cool. Can you show me?" My father's easy acceptance of all things magickal likely came from years of living with my mother and his enjoyment of…incense were we calling it? Inhaling incense daily seemed to make most people pretty easy going.

"I think so. I'm still learning. I just came out here to try it on my own, without everyone hovering over me."

"Oh, I'll leave you to it then." My dad made to leave.

"No, not you. You're not intimidating. It's hard when you've got some big magick to live up to."

"Ah. Your mother. She's a force to be reckoned with. But you don't have to live up to her magick, you know that right?"

"How so?" I squinted at him as he eased himself onto a lounge chair.

"Because her magick is hers. Yours is yours. She can't live up to yours, just like you couldn't to hers. They're just different. It's like asking a bunny rabbit to sprout wings and fly."

"Wait, are you saying she can't do what I can conceivably do? Magickally speaking?"

"Of course not. You're a sea witch, right? Your mother likes being on yachts on the water. When was the last time you saw her actually go *in* the water?"

"Um…never?"

"Exactly. She's intimidating because she's become very good at what she does. But you're very good at what you do. And in time, once you explore more of what you want and who you are – you'll be just as strong as she is in *your* particular area."

"I never really looked at it like that. She's always been so famous and all-powerful. If I didn't love her so much, she'd annoy the hell out of me." I stayed where I was, smiling at my dad, my feet digging into the sand as the cool water caressed my ankles. My dad reached down and picked up the football and turned to look over his shoulder before launching it across the yard where Hank buzzed after it.

"I'll tell ya a little secret, honey. Your mother can be wildly annoying. More than once, I've contemplated tossing her off the side of one of those fancy yachts that never serve a decent beer."

"Shut up!" My mouth dropped open in shock as I looked at him. I'd never once heard him speak poorly of my mother before.

"Your mother is an amazing and powerful woman. But she's human, Althea. We all are. Nobody's perfect. And I can be equally as annoying to her as she can be to me. But we've just decided that we choose the other person over anyone else, and you learn to work through those annoy-ances. Those are only small moments, anyways, and you can move past them. But you can't hold anyone to some standard that is impossible to meet."

"But I think that's why I fail so much – I've been holding my relationships to your standard," I said. Realization dawned on me slowly. A large part of my fear of commitment came from the fact that I viewed my parents' relationship as the most successful relationship I'd ever seen. Everyone I met, I inevitably held to that standard. Above all else, my parents genuinely enjoyed each other's company.

"Is that right? Is that's what's been going on with this Cash character? And Trace?"

"I think so." I turned and looked out over the water as I dug my toes into the sand, enjoying the squish beneath my toes.

"Then the best advice I can give you is to find a relationship based on mutual respect. At the end of the day, your mother and I deeply respect each other and we trust each other. That foundation goes a long way toward making a happy relationship."

My thoughts flashed to how Cash had continuously been dismayed by my work, while Trace had easily accepted who and what I was. Hindsight was a bitch, wasn't it?

"So. Stop expecting perfection, accept each other's flaws, trust and respect each other – and the rest falls into place?"

"Pretty much. Oh…and learn to laugh at yourself. Laughing is a pretty good thing. You know what could help you with that?"

I had a pretty good idea what my father was going to suggest and held up my hand to stop him. The last thing I needed was to cloud my mind if I was going to work on my magick.

"I'm good. Okay, so watch. Look at the wave coming in, right? I'm working on moving it."

"Go for it, sweetie."

And just like that, I settled into my power with my dad's excited exclamations urging me on to test its limits as we spent the next hour playing with what I could do. By the time my mother stormed into the backyard, I was all but crowing with delight.

"I swear to goddess, I thought I'd seen the last of that uptight viper when I'd cleaned up her last mess."

"Hi, Mom." I beamed at her and she automatically smiled at me, while my dad patted the cushion next to him for her to come sit by his side. She lowered herself and leaned into where my dad wrapped his arms around me. "Dad tells me you can be annoying."

My father slanted me a look. "Traitor."

"Oh, I'm beyond annoying." Abigail laughed and fluffed her hair. "I annoy myself at times. It's a miracle he puts up with me."

"Tough day at work, darling?" Dad brushed a kiss across mom's head.

"That Edna woman from the Star Society. Years ago I dealt with her. Amateurs messing with things they don't understand. It's going to be hell to clean up."

"You'll take care of it. You always do."

"I know. But I could be spending more one-on-one time with my beautiful daughter instead of running after wayward witches who don't know what they're dealing with."

"Consider it a bond-building activity for the two of you," Dad suggested.

"Do we need to strengthen our bonds? Are you mad at

me, honey?" My mother zeroed in on me, concern on her face.

"No, I'm not. Intimidated by you at times. But not mad. But Dad's helped me work through some of it today. Plus – look at what I'm learning." Turning, I focused on the water until I'd shaped it into a little water spout, a mini whirling ocean tornado, and laughed while Hank chased it across the beach.

"That's marvelous, darling!" Mom clapped exuberantly. "I'm so proud of you. How does it feel?"

"Honestly?" I turned, dropping the spout, and Hank whirled his head in confusion as his playtoy disappeared. "It feels good. It's something I've run from for a while now. And I can see that perhaps the anxiety of learning or being bad at it was keeping me from actually giving it an honest chance. Now that I'm working with my power in a real way, it feels great. Like, really really great. I mean, I can see why Luna says some people become intoxicated with it, but I don't think I have that kind of addictive personality. I am enjoying that little zing of power that zips through me, but I don't feel the need to bring a tsunami down on Tequila Key either."

"You'd be a terror if you did have that trait. But no, that's not you. I'm glad you're opening to this, Althea. We all grow at our own speed. I think the time is right for you to level up."

"I'm beginning to understand that. Speaking of next level – how about a burger at Lucky's?"

"Will Beau be there?" My mother brightened at seeing the person who was essentially her second child.

"He should be. He's there mid-week and weekends at his other place."

"Then, yes, I'd love to. Can we bring Hank? I hate to leave my doll-baby." Mom blew kissy noises at Hank as he stared up at her in adoration.

"Of course. Beau keeps treats for him behind the bar."

"Perfect. I could die for an ice-cold margarita."

Chapter Ten

"MAMI!" Beau exclaimed when we walked into Lucky's a while later. Beau had taken to calling my mother "Mami" in a nod to the role she played in his life. He'd been my best friend forever and ever, and my parents had welcomed him like a second son. "Mitch!"

Both my parents ran forward and embraced Beau, exclaiming over him and chattering away. Warmth spread through me as I took a little photo of the scene in my mind. These were my people, and I would always love them dearly.

"Hey."

"Trace!" I turned and leaned into Trace, wrapping my arm around his waist as he pulled me into his side for a loose hug. The last time I'd seen him we'd been dealing with corpses, and I'd meant to touch base with him after, but my parents had shown up and, well, here we were. Uncertain if he'd be angry with me for not messaging him, I looked up at him. "I'm sorry I haven't checked up on you after last week. My parents surprised me with a visit and my mom's been putting me through a magickal boot camp after she learned about all the recent events."

"Recent events seem to put things in a very clinical way, doesn't it? It sounds like a press release stating the library is closed due to recent events. I'd say it was more like catastrophes. Insanity? A total dumpster fire?" Trace's eyes creased at the corners as he smiled down at me.

"It's been…" I blew out a sigh. "Yeah, it's been ugly."

"So, magick boot camp? That sounds fun. Do you have to like run an obstacle course and explode bottles with your mind?"

I stared at Trace like he'd lost his mind.

"Um. No. Not quite like that. Is that the first thing that comes to mind?"

"Yeah, I mean, I do play a lot of war video games. Boot camp just makes me think of like intense training where you blow things up."

In all fairness, I had blown a few things up, but that hadn't been quite my intention at the time. Luckily, I was saved from answering when my parents descended upon Trace.

"Trace! You're here, too! Oh, just lovely to see you. Come, come. Join us. I've been dying for an ice-cold margarita. We'll sit at the bar so we can chat with Beau, too." Mom swooped in and dragged Trace along with her to the bar. Before perching in her chair, she scooped up Hank so he could sit on her lap. I knew her skirt was Chanel. I just knew it. And I couldn't help but laugh that she put Hank's fuzzy butt right on thousands of dollars of designer wear.

"I'd hold him for her, but she insists." My dad's eyes beamed at me as he looked at Abigail.

"She's one in a million."

"How's traveling life treating you?" Trace pulled up a chair next to me and leaned over me a bit to speak to my father. I subtly inhaled his scent – the ocean mixed with Irish spring soap – and found myself missing him terribly. Why did I always put myself in these situations where I pushed the wrong people away? Trace was one of my best friends – but he'd also been the best partner I'd ever had. Sighing, I toyed with a quartz pendant at my neck.

"Hiya, beauty. Love the hair. Can I get you a Moscow mule?" Beau asked, having returned from the other side of the bar.

"Sure. Thanks, Beau. How are things going with you?"

"Just dandy, love. Though I'm starting to think about another project."

"What? Aren't your hands full with these two restaurants?" I leaned forward and looked at Beau quizzically, and Trace automatically adjusted so he spoke over my back to my dad.

"They are. Trust me. They are. But you know me…I always love the next shiny thing. It's fun to have a project, you know? I think part of the process is buying the places and fixing them up. I love digging my hands into new things."

"You know I'll support you in whatever you want to do."

"Good, because this one may involve you as a partner."

"Excuse me? A what?" I looked at Beau in surprise,

but his attention was grabbed by a waitress coming to the other side of the bar. "Did he just say he wanted to go into business with me?"

"Sounds that way. It could be fun. Everything Beau touches turns to gold," Trace said.

"But what could I possibly do with him? I can handle the level of customer service I maintain in my job. But could you imagine me waiting tables?" I raised an eyebrow at Trace, and he laughed. Grabbing my hand, he brought it to his lips for a quick kiss and a warm sizzle of lust tingled up my arm. It was as though he'd forgotten our agreement to just be friends as we were. I wasn't surprised – we'd always had a natural chemistry with each other.

"I mean, I'd certainly enjoy watching you try to be nice to Theodore if he was a customer," Trace laughed. "But no, I don't think that's where your strengths lie."

"I guess we'll just see what he is thinking then. How have you been? I know last week was…a lot."

"I'm not going to lie, Althea. I've had some pretty gruesome nightmares since then. It would have been nice to have someone to turn to after." Trace pitched his voice low so that my father couldn't hear.

A deep breath escaped me as a mixture of tenderness and lust filled me. Turning to Trace in the night, comforting him, holding him near…it was something I *did* miss. In those moments, everything felt just right, and if we pulled the cover over our heads, nothing in the world would ever bother us again.

"I'm sorry. You should've called me. I would've come over. Or at least talked you through it. I can't say I've slept great since all of it either. I've had to leave the television on in the background to soothe me."

"Right, because screaming housewives is a soothing background noise?" Trace smiled.

"To each their own."

"Okay, I'm back with your drinks." Beau smiled at me across the bar as he slid a copper mug with a Moscow Mule across to me and a Corona to Trace. He looked good, if not as tan as usual, but his casual surfer good looks turned the heads of both men and women alike.

"I'll admit you've piqued my curiosity. Can you at least give me a hint? Otherwise, I'll obsess over your idea." I gave him my best pouty look and Beau shook his head at me and rolled his eyes in disgust.

"You never were very good at pouting, Althea. You just look like a blow fish."

"That's because I can't remember which lip I'm supposed to push out."

"The bottom." Beau sighed and looked over his shoulder, his eyes scanning the open-air bar and restaurant to make sure everyone was attended to. Lucky's ran a brisk business and people were generally happy relaxing after work with a drink under the thatched roof and looking out to the water. Seeing it was clear, he turned back to me. "I'm thinking like a wine bar and gallery. Particularly focusing on your prints."

I couldn't have made a sound if I tried. Beau had surprised me more than once in the past, but this time – well, he'd just about taken my breath away.

"Now she looks like a parrot fish with her mouth hanging open like that," Trace observed.

"I...I..."

"Or a blenny." Beau tilted his head at me and waited for me to recover my powers of speech.

"What did you do to Althea?" My mother leaned across my dad's lap and looked at me. "Did you break her?"

"I just suggested an idea of putting a little business together. A wine bar and art gallery featuring her photos."

"I..." Seriously, where had my speech gone?

"Oh, honey! That's fantastic. Your photos are amazing! What a great idea, Beau!" My mother exclaimed.

"But..." I still wasn't doing well with the talking thing.

"Althea, I know you're going to say that your work isn't good enough or whatever insecurity you want to use as an excuse. But I'm telling you, it is. Every night. Every *single* night... I get asked if your photos at the restaurant are for sale. Over and over. We don't have something like this in Tequila Key. And people love to decorate with ocean photos when they live on the coast. It's silly not to give it a go. And you love doing it. Don't you?"

I did, actually. For a long time, I'd take an early morning dive with Trace and get loads of photos for my website. But lately, what with everything going on, I hadn't been on a dive with him in quite a while. I missed it – more than I realized. And not just the diving and the photography – I missed those boat trips with Trace. It was our moment, before we tackled the day, and it had been the foundation to our friendship.

"I do." It seemed I could talk again. "I really love taking photos and I think...yes. We should do this. I'm going to say yes now before I talk myself out of this."

"Oh, honey, I'm so happy for you." My dad leaned over and kissed my cheek.

"I guess you know what that means, don't you?" Trace leaned back on his stool and took a swig of his beer.

"What?"

"I think that means we get to dive tomorrow." Trace looked at me in question.

"I want to…but…" I turned to look at my mom. "I should probably work on some other things. Tomorrow night is…"

"You go, honey. Being in the water is the best thing for you." My mother toasted me with her margarita.

"Are you sure? I should really be practicing my magicks."

"Yes, I'm sure. You'll be at your most powerful after you've been in the water. In fact, it's the best thing you can do to prep for tomorrow. I fully support this."

"Right," I blew out a breath and turned to Trace, "looks like we're going diving tomorrow."

"Why does water recharge you, exactly?" Trace squinted at me.

"Oh that? It appears I'm a sea witch."

"Of course you are," Trace laughed and I found myself grinning right back at him.

Chapter Eleven

IT HAD BEEN a while since I'd walked out to the docks when the sun was just cresting over the horizon and shooting its rays across the calm surface of the water. The fishing boats were already long gone for the morning, but other leisure boats and dive boats like Trace's were busy with getting things stocked for their guests for the day. Trace didn't have any clients until the afternoon, so he waited for me by his boat, smiling as I lugged my gear down the dock.

"Good morning."

"Good morning. You look lovely today." Trace automatically tugged the strap of my gear bag from my shoulder and stepped easily onto the boat, before turning to offer me his hand. Kicking my sandals aside, I stepped barefoot onto the deck and adjusted my body weight to the gentle sway of the boat. Trace held my hand for a moment, and I glanced up at him, a question in my eyes.

"Where's my compliment?"

"Ah, right. You look very lovely this morning, too." I

laughed as he wrinkled his nose at me and then going on impulse, I stretched up and wrapped my arms around his neck.

"And what's this? This doesn't feel like something *just friends* would do." Trace's hands had immediately come to my waist and he slid them around me, pulling my body against his.

"I have come to some recent conclusions."

"Care to share?" Trace nuzzled my neck, and I breathed in the delicious scent of him as shivers raced across my body.

"That maybe I've had everything I was looking for right in front of my face all along? And it was my own insecurity causing me to push you away out of fear?"

Trace's arms tightened at my waist, and I could feel the rhythm of his breath change.

"And what helped you to see that? What's changed your thoughts, Althea?"

"My father helped."

Trace laughed softly into my ear, and his arms loosened a bit so he could pull back and look down at me with his startlingly blue eyes.

"There's nothing a man loves more when he's feeling in the mood than to hear his girl talk about her father."

I laughed despite myself, though my body thrummed at his words about being in the mood.

"The thing is – I've always held my parents' relationship as the gold standard. And I thought they were perfect and perfect for each other. But now I've learned that apparently they annoy the shit out of each other, and both have learned to accept it."

I looked at Trace waiting for him to understand my big revelation.

"Okaaaay?" Trace asked.

"Don't you see? I was waiting for someone who didn't annoy me. Who was totally perfect. And then after a while, I realized that I wasn't perfect. So then I thought I couldn't be in a relationship until I fixed myself because that isn't fair to the other person. And now I see it's okay if we aren't totally perfect."

"So…you're saying I annoy you?"

"Of course you do. But I'm sure I annoy you as well."

"Daily," Trace agreed cheerfully and I smacked him on the arm. He pulled me tighter against him again as he laughed into my neck.

"I guess I was just holding everything to some unattainable status and after talking to my dad, who very helpfully showed me that they are not perfect, I realized what was actually important."

"Which is what?"

"Trust. Honesty. Respect. And you give all of that to me, Trace. You have always accepted me. I don't have to justify or excuse myself with you."

"You don't. I think you're amazing, Althea. Exactly as you are. Powers and all. You know that."

"Yeah, but you've also run off after other women."

"And you have with other men."

"Right, I probably shouldn't have brought that up." I leaned back and met his eyes again.

"Althea…I can't do this back and forth again. I've made it clear that I want to be with you. And I'm willing to be patient. But I can't do this on again off again thing. It's not in or out and then back in again, okay? No hokey-pokey here. If we do this again and break up for whatever reason, that's it. It's too tough on my heart, you understand?"

Trace usually always kept things light and easy, and I enjoyed our banter, but this time his tone showed me how serious he was. I knew, in my heart of hearts, if I didn't take him or us seriously this time, I'd lose him forever. He had every right to feel the way he did. It was time for me to take care with his heart.

"I understand. And I agree. No more nonsense."

"So what are you saying? Are we back together?" Joy flooded Trace's handsome face.

"We'll see," I said. I squealed as Trace picked me up and hustled me to the back of the boat and leaned me dangerously out over the water.

"I swear I'll drop you."

"Yes," I gasped. "Yes, only teasing. We're back together."

"Good," Trace said, and planted a kiss on my lips before dropping me into the water. I sputtered as I went under, furious with him, but laughed as I came up.

"You'll pay for that!"

"Just a warning. Get up here, Sea Witch. We have to get out to the reef. And, I have some questions." Trace handed me a towel as I clambered on board. The dunk in the water had woken me right up, as had our declaration to be together. Foregoing the towel, I launched myself at Trace and plastered my wet body against his as he groaned.

"I should've known you'd do this."

"Did you miss me?" I laughed as his lips met mine and for a moment we were lost to each other before we both pulled away, gasping.

"That's enough or we'll never get out on this dive. And apparently you need to charge your powers or something."

"Right. Let's go."

I helped Trace with undoing the mooring lines, and soon we were motoring out to the reef. The ocean was calm that morning, with very little chop, and we could hear each other easily over the motor.

"So, about this Sea Witch thing? Care to elaborate?"

"It appears I've got some other magick beside my psychic powers. And it stems from water. Water elements. Moving water. Perhaps calling on water creatures. I'm still learning, really." I filled him in on what I knew so far, and he listened without comment until the end.

"So, like, could you call dolphins to you?" Trace asked.

"I don't know. I could try and see," I shrugged.

"Could you imagine how amazing that would be for my dive clients?" Trace laughed and slapped his hand on the wheel. "If I could guarantee every dive they get to see a shark or dolphins. Damn, Althea. I think you need a third business."

"Oh my goddess, I hadn't even considered that. Yes, it would be amazing, but also no – I'd never exploit them like that."

"Of course not, I'd never *actually* ask you to do that."

"But, maybe, on this dive – can I try a few things? And you won't freak out?"

"I mean, it depends on what you want to try. What

should I expect? Like you can't toss me out of the water or something like that. You'll need to take our safety stops and water pressure into consideration."

"Oh, no. Nothing like that. I don't want to mess with the safety aspects of our dive. But maybe I can see if I can communicate with a few sea creatures. Or if a current is really strong, maybe I can lessen it? Stuff like that?"

"That's fine. Just always remember to keep our depth and no-deco time in consideration." Trace switched into instructor mode.

"Yes, sir." I grinned at him. He knew that I knew all the rules and always followed them, but still needed to repeat them to me. Habit, I suppose.

Once we'd reached the reef and hooked the boat to the permanent mooring there, we quickly geared up, moving harmoniously in silence around each other as we did a buddy check. Grabbing my camera, I did a giant stride off the back of the boat and into the water, bobbing gently at the surface as I turned around to let Trace know I was safe. Once he'd entered the water, we signaled to each other to descend, and I breathed in as joy filled my entire being.

It had been a few months since I'd gone on a dive, and I truly had been missing it. The ocean embraced me like it was welcoming me home and happiness pulsed through me as I floated gently down to the reef. Once there, I hovered over the reef and studied the coral, watching the fish dart beneath sea fans and peer out at me as I swam slowly past. For a while, I spent my time taking easy shots of the fish, just enjoying having a camera in my hand again and playing with my settings as we lazily swam over the reef. A porcupine pufferfish floated up to me, and I grinned into my regulator, remembering how Beau had said I looked like a blowfish yesterday. Firing off a few shots, I continued on until we swam closer to a sandy patch.

Signaling to Trace to follow me over the sand, I paused once we were far enough away from the reef. I wasn't entirely sure what my powers would look like underwater and the corals already had enough stress placed on them from cruise ships and other environmental stressors. I certainly didn't need to add to it. Trace watched me, his eyes curious through his mask, as I floated in place and thought about what to do.

I suppose I could try for a turtle, I thought. But I'd need to do it in a way that it would be their choice to come to me. I didn't want to mess with any animal's free will. This was the line that Luna had been talking about crossing. She wanted me to work harmoniously with nature and not in a forceful manner. With that in mind, I spent some time calling the elements and then I sent out a gentle request to the turtles in the area, letting them know that I was there and if they felt like coming to say hello – I would hang out for a little while longer. Keeping my eye on my dive computer for my air, I signaled to Trace to wait.

It couldn't have been more than two minutes when the first turtle crested the reef and swam lazily toward us, his dappled shell a mosaic of greens and browns. I smiled at him, noting the awareness in his eyes, and waved one hand at him. Pulling my camera up, I took a few shots as he circled us, joy filling me that my power seemed to be working.

Trace grabbed my arm and squeezed tightly. Turning, I looked over my shoulder and almost dropped my regulator from my mouth. A dark mass moved towards us. A mass of turtles. There had to be at least fifty in the group, cruising across the reef and swimming toward us. It was like all the turtles had come out to play in one mass turtle rave, and I looked at Trace in shock.

I could see his eyes crinkling in laughter behind his mask and then he made a stop motion with his hand for me to slow the incoming turtles. Of course! I hadn't thought to end my magickal signal. I was probably still sending out the invitation. Quickly closing that intention off, I brought my camera up and took picture after picture of this incredible grouping of hawksbill, green, and loggerhead turtles. I mean, Beau had wanted new photos, right? Well, he was certainly going to get some. A once-in-a-lifetime experience, that was.

Gently thanking the turtles and sending them my love, I waved goodbye as they split off, some following others, and moved on with their day. It had been an incredible encounter, and my heart raced with happiness at seeing so many healthy and happy turtles.

But I could certainly see where a power like this could be exploited for the bad. If I could call the sea life to me, imagine what shark fin terrorists or whaling companies would do if they had someone like me. I shuddered to think about it.

Signaling it was time to go, Trace grabbed my hand and held it as we ascended and waited during our safety stop at fifteen feet. Trace crinkled his eyes at me and then grabbed me in his arms, spinning me like we were on the dance floor, and I laughed, loving him and loving my life. My mother had been right about the ocean recharging me – but so had my decision to give Trace a serious chance.

For the first time in forever, I felt actually powerful and like I could tackle whatever came my way.

Watch out, Edna, I thought. *I'm coming for you.*

Chapter Twelve

MY HOUSE HAD BEEN DESIGNATED as the meeting point to review our plan of attack prior to sunset that evening. Luna, and my parents and I were already there – my father quietly bustling around in the kitchen as he made one of his favorite comfort foods: chicken pot pie.

"It's so nice to bum around in a kitchen again." My dad diced boiled chicken on a cutting board. "All these fancy yachts and hotels don't let you do a single thing for yourself. One time I wanted to just make a piece of toast and I got booted out of the kitchen and was served a platter of pastries."

"I like pastries."

"So do I. But sometimes you just want a piece of toast. A nice crusty bread, toasted up with some melted butter? Simple, yet perfect. And then I was forced to eat croissants. With chocolate inside."

"You poor thing. I really feel for you and how awful it must be to live such a luxurious lifestyle," I teased.

"I know, I know." Dad grinned and began on the

carrots. "But that's the problem with luxury. After a while it loses its novelty. It becomes expected and you don't see it anymore. I'm glad to be back here. I missed being able to cook my own food. Control the music playlist. Not have to dress a particular way for dinner. There's certain people who are meant for that lifestyle, but I'm not one of them."

"Do you talk to mom about this stuff?" I snagged a carrot from the board and crunched down on it, leaning against the counter as I studied him. Bob Dylan played in the background and my dad had tied on an apron sporting a Boston Terrier in a bow tie.

"I do. It's part of why we didn't take our next trip and came here instead. We're in the process of negotiating a six-month agreement."

"And what does that look like exactly?"

"Six months out of the year we go to a spot of mine and six months out of the year we travel the way she wants."

I immediately tried to picture my mom in a camper van careening around the States to the national parks and just...couldn't see it.

"What are you thinking for your spot?"

"I want a little cottage somewhere. We pack up and go so much right now and have seen so many amazing things that I want some quiet where I can work on some of my music. I've been eyeing a cottage on the cliffs of Ireland, actually. West Coast."

I could instantly picture it – Mom charming the villagers and Dad puttering about in a wooly sweater.

"I'd visit you there. It sounds like the perfect contrast to here."

A knock sounded at my door, setting Hank off in a cacophony of barking, and I crossed the room to open the door to Miss Elva, resplendent in black sequins with Rosita floating over her shoulder.

"I still don't know why you think sequins is appropriate breaking and entering attire," I said.

"They're black, aren't they?" Miss Elva blew kisses to Hank and breezed past me with a huge tote bag in hand.

"Dad, there's a ghost here now just so you know." I smiled at Rosita, who was hovering over my father and observing what he was doing.

"Is there?" My dad looked around and squinted through his glasses. "How cool. Tell him I said hello."

"*Her* name is Rosita and she can hear you."

"Well, hello, Rosita. I'd invite you for dinner, but I suppose I can't really cook for you, can I?"

Rosita glanced at me, her mouth hanging open. "I don't know when a man has ever offered to cook for me. How charming."

"Yes, he's a regular Lothario."

"I like the look of him. He's quite handsome." Besotted, Rosita moved around to the other side of the counter so she could stare at my father while he cooked, but he was oblivious to the new admirer he'd acquired.

"He's taken, Rosita."

"Hush. A girl can dream, can't she?"

"What's that, Althea?" My dad looked around in confusion.

"Rosita thinks it was very sweet of you to invite her to dinner. It wasn't something that happened often for her during her time."

"Never. Not once," Rosita pouted.

"Poor girl. That's a shame. Why wouldn't a nice lad take her for dinner?"

"She was a Madam," I said cheerfully. "I imagine she terrified the nice lads."

"It's true…" Rosita shook her head and laughed. "The nice ones were too shy to use my services and the others… well…they had their uses. None of which was cooking for me."

"I'm sure she has some fascinating stories to share," my father said. "But her career choice shouldn't preclude her from getting asked to dinner."

My father, ladies and gentlemen. The original feminist.

"Can I keep him?" Rosita looked at me, her eyes huge.

"You certainly may not." Abigail stepped inside the house, looking as subdued as she could in black leather leggings and a loosely draped, off the shoulder black t-shirt. "This one's mine, Rosita. Find someone else's husband to poach."

"But he's so dreamy…" Rosita sighed.

"Which is why I picked him. He's mine. Back off," Abigail warned.

"I'm just looking," Rosita promised. "Plus he invited me to dinner. It's rude to turn me away."

"I'm sure you can join a dinner elsewhere," Abigail said.

"Ladies, ladies. Please. No need to argue," My dad said. "Rosita, you are, of course, welcome to dinner. But this lovely lady of mine stole my heart years ago and I'm a one-woman man." My dad seemed slightly bemused by the current discussion – as though he couldn't believe he'd ended up being fought over by a Madam ghost and his wife.

"You're a lucky woman, Abigail."

"I count my blessings every day. Mitchell is the best thing that's ever happened to me."

At that, my father dropped the knife and rounded the counter to put his arms around my mother and dip her in a doozy of a kiss. Even though they were my parents, my heart still did a happy little shiver when I saw it. Maybe I was just in a good mood after my morning with Trace or maybe I just needed to see that love lasted.

"I swear I'd swoon if I could," Rosita said, a dreamy look on her face.

"That's enough canoodling, you two. We've got an Edna to take down," Miss Elva called from the back porch and my parents broke their kiss. Mom and I shuffled outside and plopped onto the couch next to each other. Luna sat, reviewing the notebook she'd pulled out the other day with the Celtic knot on the front, and Miss Elva stood before her big tote bag.

"I decided we needed a theme," Miss Elva said. She dug around in her tote, and then handed me some clothes.

"A theme? For what, exactly?" I looked up at her in surprise.

"Well, if the Seven Star Sister Society or whatever they are called – like honestly couldn't they shorten that name? Anyways, child, if *they* get a name, we can have a name."

"We're naming us *now*?" I looked at Luna who just shrugged.

"It's not uncommon to name your coven as it does help bring unity and power," Luna said. Tonight she wore simple black jeans, a black long-sleeved t-shirt, and black sneakers. I rarely saw her wear black, but no matter what she attired herself in, she glowed.

"Oh, so now we're a coven? Right. Got it. Okay, Miss Elva – what did you pick for us?"

"That's damn right, we are. Go on – open it up!" Miss Elva danced in her sequins and waited for us to unfold our shirts.

"Is that…" I tilted my head at the hot pink design on the black shirt.

"Ovaries and fallopian tubes?" Abigail tilted her head at the design.

"OG?" I looked at the large pink lettering under the ovaries.

"Yes! Ovary Gang!" Miss Elva clapped her hands.

I just blinked at her while Luna started laughing.

"Very progressive. I like it." My mother stood and stripped off her shirt and pulled the OG shirt over her head. I had to admit, it looked pretty cute. It was cut in a similar scoop neck off the shoulder slouchy look like the other t-shirt my mother had just been wearing and the hot pink lettering popped. Plus, the design of the uterus and ovaries wasn't immediately recognizable the way the t-shirt slouched, and the fabric folded.

"And! I have hats!" Miss Elva handed out black trucker hats with hot pink OG written on the front. "Abigail, you'll have to cover that bright hair of yours."

"That's a good point." My mother put the hat on and tucked her hair in a low bun at her neck. She looked impossibly chic, and I once again admired that no matter what Abigail put on, she pulled it off.

The rest of us quickly changed into our OG attire – well, Miss Elva kept her sparkles on but put her trucker hat on – and then called for Mitchell to come take a picture of us.

"Oh, I love this. Very edgy, ladies." My dad squinted at the phone and then back up at us. "Did I take the picture? It didn't make the clicking sound."

"Just hit the button a bunch. I have it on silent." I laughed as my dad took a few more photos and then returned to his cooking. Plopping back down, I smiled at the women around me. A warm glow had infused me, and I felt surrounded by love and happiness, having the people I most cared about in the world around me. Perhaps that was all that was needed to have a coven, I realized.

"I love you ladies. So much."

The women all turned to me with surprise on their faces.

"Are you going to cry?" Miss Elva looked at me with fear on her face.

"Nope. I promise!" I laughed at the relief that crossed her face. "I just realized how nice it is to be together like this."

"You're particularly emotional today," Luna eyed me. "How did that dive with Trace go this morning?"

"Love lives later, ladies. We have a lot to go over." Abigail clapped her hands and I shot Luna a look promising to fill her in on the details later.

"We do. Okay, now that the OG is ready to rock – let's get down to brass tacks. I've made some notes." Luna held up her notebook. "And I am particularly concerned about Althea's vision of a sprite."

"They are tricky," Abigail agreed.

"Okay, so first up – I got the plans for Edna's house and the security code numbers for her system." Miss Elva shocked me by rolling out an architectural map of the house which showcased the layout of bedrooms, kitchen, and bathrooms.

"How in the world did you get these?"

"I used to sleep with the permits guy. He's fun, though plays by the rules. I always enjoyed trying to make him loosen up a bit." Miss Elva paused and drifted away for a moment, a little smile on her face.

"And the codes? Did you sleep with the security system guy, too?" I snapped a finger in front of Miss Elva's face to bring her back to the here and now.

"Nope. That one you have Rosita to thank for."

We all looked to where Rosita smiled from her perch on the back of the couch.

"Edna can't see me. It was quite easy to hang over her shoulder when she punched the code in."

"Brilliant." I shot a smile at Rosita whose grin widened at my praise.

"Basically, we have a couple options. We can enter here or here, but I think through this side door and straight to the backyard makes the most sense." Miss Elva tapped the map and we all bent over and studied the various entrances.

"Should we split up?" I asked, looking around. "Just in case? Would that increase our odds of stopping the spell?"

"Not a bad idea," Mom agreed. "Luna and I can sneak in the west side of the house and you three can go in the east."

Rosita beamed again at being included. Aww, I was getting sappy, wasn't I? I just loved all this feminine power energy going on right now.

"Once we're in, we basically either want to prevent or dismantle the spell if it is already in progress," Luna said. "Dismantling is essentially like throwing a wet blanket over a fire. We want to smother it and then break it apart as fast as we can. There are a few different ways to do that. I've created a little printout with the quickest ones for everyone to look over."

I interpreted the undertone of that to mean for *me* to look over as the other two women barely glanced at it.

"And if nothing works?" I asked.

"Then we deal with what comes next. Remember, Althea. Our first rule of thumb is to harm none. You aren't trying to hurt Edna." Luna shot a look at Miss Elva.

"It's not my fault she ate prunes for lunch." Miss Elva shrugged.

"We just want to stop magick from being improperly done."

"And what about this sprite that I saw?"

"That's my biggest concern. If things go awry tonight and a sprite manifests, we're going to have chaos on our hands," Luna shook her head.

"Why?"

"Oh, they're feisty little buggers. Irish ones are at least. They aren't fully corporeal, and they flit in and out of physical form. They love water and use it to bounce around to other places and realms. They love chaos. The more the better. And parties. Destruction. Loud noises.

And because they can bounce in and out of our realm once manifested, it is really tricky to subdue one."

"Althea, you're certain you saw a sprite? Wreaking havoc?"

"He was turning on Chief Thomas's police sirens and chugging a beer."

"Goddess help us," Abigail said grimly.

Chapter Thirteen

EDNA'S HOUSE was located at the end of a quiet treelined street that hugged the waterline. Unlike most streets in Tequila Key, there was ample space between the houses providing a level of privacy that I could see being attractive to many. I mean, considering my neighbors had about given up on having any semblance of normalcy with me living on their street, I was surprised that more of them hadn't moved out to a place like this. Granted, it was a further drive from downtown, but I could see the appeal of this neighborhood – particularly if you wanted to do spell work.

We'd all piled into Miss Elva's flamingo-pink Land Rover and now she pulled it to the side of the street and parked.

"I still don't know why we took your car. You're the only person with a flamingo pink car in Tequila Key," I pointed out as we unbuckled our seat belts.

"Edna already knows we're coming," Miss Elva glanced back at me. "She may not be great with magick, but she's not stupid, child. I could park in her damn driveway and we'd still be dealing with what we're about to deal with."

"Point taken." Miss Elva was right. Edna was very much aware that we weren't happy with whatever ritual she was about to partake in.

"I'd be aware of any little boobytraps she might have laid out for us," Luna pointed out.

Miss Elva dug in her tote bag, which I swear had a black hole at the bottom and she just reached into the void and pulled out what she needed, and then tossed something in front of us down the street while muttering a few words. In seconds, a light violet hue crept along the ground, a softly lit cloud of smoke that spread out and encompassed the entire area all the way to Edna's house.

"Anything lit up orange is meant to cause us harm," Miss Elva said.

"There." Luna pointed to an orange spot in the road and we carefully made our way around it.

"Nails?" I squinted in the darkness.

"Simple, yet effective. A nail through the foot would hurt," Mom pointed out.

"Another over here," Miss Elva whispered and pointed. Slowly we made our way to the house, dodging various traps until we came to one that hovered in the air in front of us. "Oh, that bitch."

"What is it?" I tilted my head at the lines.

"Barbed wire. She wanted to clothesline us. But she also hung it so closely together that a fuller figured woman such as myself can't squeeze through it."

"No problem." Abigail reached into her purse and

pulled out a small bolt cutter and neatly snipped the wires. My eyes widened.

"You carry bolt cutters? How do they even fit in your bag?"

My mother just smiled, and we stepped over the fallen wires.

"That was real nasty of her. We could've been seriously hurt if we walked into those. What if it caught in our eye?" Miss Elva fumed. I didn't point out that we were trespassing on her property, so she technically did have the right to string up barbed wire anywhere she wanted.

"Shhh." Luna waved her hands at us and lowered her voice to a whisper. "It's time to split up. Meet back at the car if everything falls apart." Miss Elva had given us each a key to the car in case one of us needed to be the getaway driver.

Miss Elva, Rosita, and I split up and made our way around the side of the house to the door where we were supposed to enter. The house was essentially a one-story open square surrounding a large courtyard. I imagined it was actually quite lovely as each room in the house could open up into the courtyard. It also likely provided Edna with the privacy she was craving when it came to casting her spells.

"Okay, let's do this. Are you ready, Popcorn?" Miss Elva eyed me. She'd made us choose nicknames for our team. Somehow I'd been assigned my favorite snack food.

"Yes, Sparkles. I am."

Miss Elva held a finger to her lips, and I rolled my eyes as she bent over in the darkness and muttered a spell over the lock in the door. In seconds, we were in the house, and I marveled once more at the depth of power that Miss Elva had at her disposal. Honestly, I'd be a menace if I could do half the things she could do. I was too nosey to hold that much power. I waited while Miss Elva keyed in the code on the pad. We both held our breath. When the pad flashed green, I let out my breath and flashed Rosita a thumbs-up.

Turning, Miss Elva and I took one step down the hallway and I drew up short when she stopped.

"What's wrong?" I peered over Miss Elva's shoulder.

"Cats." Miss Elva whispered back.

"So? It's just a cat. Go past it."

"Cats. Plural." Miss Elva hissed, and I moved to the side of her and stopped.

"Oh."

"Go on then, Popcorn. You so sure of yourself and all?"

"I mean…I'm more of a dog person, really. I think you should go."

Miss Elva had mentioned that Edna liked cats. What she'd failed to mention was that she collected them. Both alive and dead it seemed. At least nine living ones sat in the hallway, tilting their heads at us. Shelves lined the wall of the hall and were decorated with cat statues, cat memorabilia, and…

"Are those…stuffed cats?" And I didn't mean cute cat stuffed animals.

"Child…sho look that way to me." Miss Elva glared at the shelves. "Now who is going to do that to their nice cat?"

"I really can't say. I feel like it would be hard to look at day in and day out. I mean…wouldn't a nice photograph of the deceased do?" I cringed at the shelves. "Also, why are none of the cats on the floor moving? They're just…staring."

"I don't know. I don't do cats."

"I mean…if they were dogs, they'd run over to greet us. Or attack, I suppose. But they're just…watching us."

We eyed the feline army for a bit, unsure of our next move.

"Do you think they'll jump on us?" I asked.

"I mean…they're Edna's cats. So, probably?"

"Aren't cats easy to scare? Like the scaredy cat thing? Isn't that why they've got a reputation?" I asked.

"Oh right. Okay." Miss Elva leaned over. "Boo!"

The cats blinked at her.

"Not quite what I was thinking there, Sparkles."

"Okay, then, Popcorn – you go for it."

"Um…" I dug in my purse until I found a bottle cap that Trace had given me to dispose of. I could throw something at them. Holding it up, I tossed it at the cats. Two of them looked down and began batting it between their paws.

"Oh sure. Give them a toy. Nice going, Popcorn."

"What's your bright idea then, Sparkles?" I glared at Miss Elva.

"They seem harmless enough. I think we just walk through them. Look – they're playing so nicely with your bottle cap. I'm sure it will be fine."

"Sure. You first." I motioned for Miss Elva to go.

"I insist, Popcorn. I'll need to get your back if they attack."

"Oh, you two are ridiculous." Rosita sighed. Turning, she grew in size and then raced at the cats, screaming a banshee scream. The cats simultaneously jumped four feet in the air and then each one lunged in different directions. One bounced off my chest and I screeched, but it was gone before I could do anything. Another landed on Miss Elva and its claws got stuck in her sequins. The two struggled together, mutually horrified, both letting out little mewls of distress. Miss Elva got her hands around the gyrating creature and tugged, trying to rip it from her shirt.

"Hold on," I hissed. I wasn't going to laugh. I swear I wasn't going to laugh. I pressed my lips firmly together and breathed through my nose, bending over to grab one of the flailing cat's paws to unhook it from the sequins.

A snort escaped.

"That better not be laughter, Popcorn."

"Nope." A tiny squeal escaped me as I worked to keep the laughter inside. A tear raced down my cheek and I kept my head bent, working to release the scared cat's paws from Miss Elva.

"It sounds like you're laughing. It'll be the last time you pop, if you get what I'm saying, Popcorn? You understand me? You'd better not be laughing at my expense."

"I'm not…" I wheezed, tears streaming down my face and finally extradited the terrified cat and sent it careening down the hallway. "It's allergies. Cat hair and all that." I wiped my eyes while Miss Elva studied me.

"Hmpf. I suppose that makes sense. Allergies are tricky."

"They are. Can't. Do. Cats." I wiped my eyes vigorously and did everything I could to keep another snort from escaping. Finally getting myself under control, I crept forward, past the scary dead cat shelves and around the corridor that should lead us to the backyard.

"Hot mama!"

Miss Elva and I both jumped at a raucous voice that sounded at our ears.

"What the hell?" I shrieked.

"Ohhh mama. Hot, hot, hot."

"It's a bird." Miss Elva hissed, her nails digging into my arm where she'd latched on at the first scream.

"What the hell is this? The house of horrors?" I asked, leaning backwards from where the bird danced on its perch.

"Why are its wings up like that?" Miss Elva looked at the bird whose wings were held back from his body like he was raising his arms in the air. He hopped back and forth from foot to foot and bobbed his head.

"Hot mama!" The bird screeched again.

"Is he calling me hot?" Miss Elva automatically preened, blowing a kiss to the bird.

"Seriously? You're flirting with a bird."

"Well, he thinks I'm cute. You have to be nice to your admirers."

"How do you know he's not talking to me?" I asked, turning to glare at Miss Elva.

"Child, you know birds like all the shiny things."

"Birds like popcorn, too," I muttered.

"Don't go on and get all bent out of shape now. He's just calling it like he sees it."

"HOT MAMA!" The bird screeched even louder,

increasingly his decibel level significantly, and I grabbed Miss Elva's arm.

"Go! He's screaming too loudly. He's alerting her. Go!" I shoved Miss Elva down the hallway, and she ran ahead of me, her sparkles picking up all the light in the hall as she disco-balled her way out to the courtyard. There, we skidded to a stop and ducked behind a statue of several naked women reaching to the sky.

"Well, this is a choice," Miss Elva said, studying the sculpture.

"Shhh," I hissed at Miss Elva, and we peered around the statue to see what was happening in the middle of the courtyard.

Six women – all sky-clad – held hands in a circle around a large cauldron. They danced slowly around it, humming, while the seventh naked woman – Edna – stepped toward the cauldron. I averted my eyes to her nakedness and instead focused on what she had in her hand.

"Your necklace."

"That bitch. She'd better not throw that in the cauldron," Miss Elva hissed.

"Well, get working on your magick because it's about to start."

"Luna was supposed to throw a spell first. I don't see her magick yet."

"Well, just give it a moment then…I trust Luna."

But the words were barely out of my mouth before Edna chanted something and tossed the necklace into the boiling cauldron. Miss Elva howled in rage and shot off a blast of magick, breaking through the circle and intercepting the light that shot out of the cauldron and toward the sky. Edna whirled, fury etched on her face, as explosions shot from the cauldron. The Star Sisters dove onto the lawn, while Edna reached in the cauldron and then raced from the courtyard. Luna and Abigail burst into the courtyard, shock etched on their faces, as a tiny creature hopped to the edge of the cauldron, beat his chest with his fists, shrieked what I could only presume was a war cry and darted off in the other direction. Luna and Abigail gave chase while Miss Elva was halfway across the courtyard after Edna. Whirling, I realized I had to stay with my team and took off, bounding across the courtyard, leaping over the naked prone bodies of the huddled Star Sister Society.

As dismantling spells went, I'd say we'd more likely destroyed than dismantled. But hey, who am I to judge, right?

Chapter Fourteen

I CAUGHT up with Miss Elva as she ran through the living room and followed her around the house and out the door to the garage where Edna had hopped onto her golf cart. You know the ones that senior citizens drive in Florida? It was *that* type of golf cart. Except she hadn't painted hers all fancy yet or clearly added much speed to it, as she slowly backed from the garage. The loud beeping from the reverse alarm on the golf cart made me look at the ceiling of the garage in disbelief for a moment.

"Edna! You get back here," Miss Elva shouted. Edna whipped the golf cart around and began her getaway.

"Back off, fattie! You ruined my spell."

"Who you calling fat, you old scarecrow?" Miss Elva huffed along, barely catching up with the golf cart, and Edna put the pedal to the metal.

"I hate you," Edna hissed.

"You stole my necklace!" Miss Elva panted, barely keeping pace as the golf cart sedately made its way down the road.

"It wasn't yours. It was destined for greatness. We were supposed to bring Goddess Mintaka down to us with that necklace. You've ruined everything." The golf cart whirred softly down the pavement, the only other sound Miss Elva's labored breathing as she kept pace. I walked behind them, too entertained to interfere.

"I know you've still got it. I saw you reach in the cauldron. Give it back, you old bat."

"Who you calling old, you fat pig? You can't even keep up!" Edna clenched the steering wheel tighter and slammed her foot down, increasing the speed minutely.

"At least I don't need an old folks golf cart to get around," Miss Elva huffed.

"I don't need one. I just have one because I like it," Edna shouted.

"Yeah, right. This thing isn't even street legal. And where are the stripes? I would have put racing stripes on mine."

"Racing stripes are for people with no taste. I'm classy," Edna shouted.

"Says the woman driving naked down the road in her golf cart. Ever hear of waxing, Edna?" Miss Elva was now running directly beside the golf cart, close enough to grab the wheel and I picked up the pace, worried that she'd hurt herself.

"Give me my necklace."

"Fine, come and get it, Elva. I've tucked it discretely away."

"If you think I won't go up your cooch and pull it out…" Miss Elva threatened and my eyebrows about hit my hairline.

"There will be no cooch invasions!" I shouted just as a squeal of tires sounded behind me. Whirling, I saw my mother at the wheel of Miss Elva's Land Rover.

"Get in. We've got bigger problems than Edna now."

"Miss Elva. Get in the car."

"She's got my necklace!" Miss Elva shouted.

"Now!" Abigail barked in a tone that left no room for disobedience. Even Edna slowed her golf cart at my mother's tone. Reluctantly, Miss Elva turned but not before she reached out and slapped Edna lightly across the face. The old woman squawked much like her parrot and I bit back a laugh.

"I can't believe you just did that," I said to Miss Elva as I crawled in the backseat.

"I can't tell you how much I hate her," Miss Elva huffed, bringing her heart rate down, as she fumed in the backseat. "She knows that necklace is mine. And like she'd even be inventive enough to put it in her cooch."

"Maybe she was trying something new."

"Women like her don't try something new. They repeat the same thing over and over until they die – bitter and dried up – because they never decided to change things up."

"Ladies. That was…" Abigail shot us a look over her shoulder as she drove away, shaking her head as she fell silent.

"I'm sorry," Miss Elva said. "That one was my fault. I knew I was supposed to wait for Luna's magick. But it just infuriated me that she tossed the necklace in like it meant nothing."

"What took you ladies so long to get inside? We were

waiting forever for the sign from you," Luna looked over her shoulder.

"Oh. Right. I was supposed to let you know we'd gotten to the courtyard. I forgot that part when I saw the necklace." Miss Elva shook her head. It was rare for her to be sloppy with magick, so I was surprised she'd forgotten Luna's cue.

"It's okay. I mean…we've got a problem on our hands. A big one. But we're used to that. I'm sorry, Miss Elva. I know you were really attached to that necklace," Luna said.

"It's stupid, really. Like…I know that it's just an inanimate object and I can find other necklaces. But that one just…I don't even know. Entranced me? It's like I'm besotted with it. I can't say why really. It's just meant to be mine."

"Then we'll figure out a way to get it…or restore it." I reached out and squeezed her hand.

"And rid it of coochie germs," Abigail promised, and I bit my lip to keep from laughing at my mother saying the word "coochie."

"Ladies. If we can focus?" Luna asked, her voice tense as she paged through a book in her lap.

"I'm assuming that little ferocious man was *the* sprite?" I asked.

"That it was. Did he look close to your vision?" Luna glanced back at me and I felt the tension knot in my stomach.

"He did."

"Well, now, that's no good." Miss Elva sighed. "Sprites are fun if you get them drunk, but it's best to do so in a forest or something. In a city, well, they're more than likely to burn it down."

"Um, when did you ever go drinking with a sprite?" I turned to Miss Elva.

"Ah, well, ages ago. I did one of those backpack around Europe summers."

I couldn't have been more shocked than if Miss Elva had told me she played the accordion and made bratwurst as a hobby.

"I'm sorry – what? You backpack?"

"Well, technically, no. I found some lovely gentlemen who were more than happy to carry my backpack for me in exchange for…"

"We know. We know," I said, holding my hands to my ears. Honestly there was only so much a woman could take.

"What? I was going to say money." Miss Elva grinned at me.

"Liar," I muttered.

"You're right. I had a lot of fun with those two. Inventive guys, they were."

"Ahhh, I think everyone should have a backpacking through Europe kind of summer." My mother sighed and my eyes almost bulged out of my head. Okay, now I'd heard too much.

"Please. The sprite. Can we stay on the topic of the sprite?" I begged.

"Yes, well. This one was Irish. And I met him by a stone circle. I gave him one of my beers and we hung out for a while. I mean, it was tricky, because he got drunk fast, what with being so small and all, and then he just wanted to sing or pick fights with people."

"Sounds familiar. I think I met a few sprites myself in my college days," Abigail laughed.

"But what I did learn is they love music. And they love to fight. So…"

"We need to find the nearest pub and see if we can sing him into a trap?" I asked.

"Pretty much."

"Lovely, I'm sure this won't be problematic at all."

Chapter Fifteen

"FIRST OF ALL, I don't even know why it's our obligation to find this thing. It's Edna's problem. She invited the damn thing into our realm with her half-assed spell." Miss Elva peered in the window. "Can we stop at this food truck? All that running has made me hungry."

I didn't think it would be in my best interest to point out she'd only run a block. But if I was being honest – I also wanted snacks.

"I mean, we'll need fuel, right?" I leaned forward and looked at the truck we were pulling up on. "Oh, tacos."

"Fine. But I'd like the record to note that we are all responsible for capturing this sprite." Luna turned in her seat and gave us both a look. "While we can't know the outcome of Edna's spell, it was our interference that caused it to go awry. We now have a duty to protect the citizens of Tequila Key."

"My interference," Miss Elva said quietly. "It was my mistake. I don't make them often. And I don't apologize often. But I have no problem owning my mistakes. I swear this necklace has a hold on me. If you all just want to get tacos and go home, I'll keep after the sprite. I can clean up my own messes."

We all looked at her askance.

"Listen up, Sparkles." I put on my stern voice. "Do you think the Ovary Gang just drops one of their..." I paused as I thought about it. What would they drop? It couldn't be an ovary because there were more than two of us. I looked around helplessly.

"Eggs?" Luna supplied, a cringey look on her face.

"Right. You don't think we'll just drop one of our eggs and..." Again, I wasn't sure where to go from here. "Never mind. Listen. We're in this together. How many times have you ladies helped me? You could've just left me to suffer the consequences of my actions. But you didn't. Time and time again, you've showed me what friendship means. Even if one of us screws up – we're there for each other."

"I feel like we need a special handshake," Mom said.

"Um." I held my hands in two circles over where my ovaries were. "Like a sign? A gang sign?"

"Sure, that will work." Miss Elva's smile broke through her worried face and she held up her hands in two circles over her own ovaries. "Ovary Gang – unite!"

"Ovary Gang – let's riot!" I tried out and the women looked at me. I shrugged.

"Ovary Gang – sisters for life!" My mom shouted and we all cheered.

"So...tacos?" Miss Elva eyed the truck hopefully and we all left the Land Rover and put our orders in. Once we each had our own variety of street taco – carne asada for me – we leaned against the hood of the car and looked out to the street. The night was quiet, as was usual for mid-week in Tequila Key. Well, almost any night in Tequila Key, really.

"I can't believe I'm saying this, but this taco is delicious," Mom said. She looked curiously at the taco in her hand. "It's been ages since I've eaten any street food." The way she said street food implied that the food was literally made on the dirty street.

"You're getting mighty fancy these days, aren't you Abigail?" Miss Elva asked.

"I suppose, a bit. You know how it is, Elva. You get caught up with the next high-paying client. It's hard to say no to trips on fancy boats or classy hotels in far-flung destinations."

"But you need balance. That's not reality," Miss Elva said.

"It is for some. But not mine, no. I suppose it could be, but Mitchell would never be happy with that extravagant lifestyle. He tolerates it because he loves me, but I think anywhere that has constant staff attending to your needs drives him nuts."

"He said he wants to do a six-month kind of thing. Six months at a little house somewhere settled in and six months traveling. Do you think you'll like that?" I asked.

"I do. We've been looking at some spots in Ireland, actually. And you know how much I tap into my Celtic side. It would be a perfect fit." Mom slanted a look at me. "And you could come out and stay a while."

Instantly I felt the cold refreshing breezes of the

Atlantic Ocean pouring over my face and my heart swelled at the idea.

"I would love nothing more." We all looked up as sirens sounded in the distance.

"Well, enough of this cozy chat. I think we know where our sprite has run off to," Luna sighed.

"That's actually a much easier way of finding him," Miss Elva pointed out, wiping off her hands with a napkin. "Just grab a snack and wait for the next disturbance."

"It beats driving around aimlessly," I agreed and hopped in the back seat of the car.

"Is that coming from the fire station?" Mom asked as she took the wheel again. Miss Elva didn't seem to mind her driving the Land Rover, and I was more than happy to have someone other than Miss Elva at the wheel. Miss Elva drove like she'd just robbed a bank and needed to make it over the border before she got caught.

"I wouldn't be surprised. The lure of loud sirens and shiny big trucks might be too much to resist," Miss Elva said.

"Are sprites like leprechauns? They kind of sound like they have similar characteristics," I asked.

"Sprites, fairies, leprechauns – they are all kind of different and yet share some similar qualities. I think the biggest qualities those three carry that overlap is that they can be tricksters. They're mercurial. Remember that," Luna said, paging through the book in her lap.

"Have you found anything in particular that will help with him?" I leaned forward as we neared the fire station.

"Not yet, no. Just various spells that can help mitigate the damage he does. What I need is a proper containment spell. We basically need to track him and then subdue him enough to pop him back over into his realm again." Luna looked up as we neared the sirens. "It's going to be a long night."

"Or days," Miss Elva put in. "We'd be lucky to contain him in a day. They also like a lot of sleep. So, he'll tuck himself away, just somewhere in the in-between veil and we won't be able to reach him. That's part of why they are so tricky."

"Days? Oh." I mentally readjusted what we were dealing with here. I'd thought to capture the little bugger and be back home – perhaps with a quick visit from Trace – and on my way to sleep before too long.

"Saddle up, OGs. The fire station is down this road," Miss Elva said, and I just looked at her, giving her a small shake of my head. "What? Saddle up doesn't work?"

"I mean…it's an option. I don't know…" I shrugged.

"Strap it on?" My mom considered and I buried my face in my hands.

"No, I'm thinking that's not quite the route we want to take either," Luna said quickly, biting back a laugh.

"Hit 'em hard?" Miss Elva asked.

"Nope. Nope. Nope." I gasped, trying to hold down my laughter.

"Take 'em down?" Luna asked and we all turned to look at her. She threw her hands up. "What? Like…take the bad guy down. But also like you could take them down there…you know."

"We know!" I said emphatically. "Trust me. We know."

"I like it," my mother decided.

"Come on, OGs!" Miss Elva squealed as we pulled up to the fire station with a screech of the tires. "Let's take 'em down."

"Down there." I said under my breath. So I could be immature, okay?

Luna winked at me and then we all jumped out of the Land Rover to survey the situation at the fire station. It was absolute chaos. Big burly firemen dressed only in their underwear were running screaming, their hands in the air, and looking wildly over their shoulders. Every fire truck siren was blaring, and lights were flashing intermittently. Some men tried to turn off the trucks, only to be tossed away as though they weighed less than a fluffy bunny.

"Let's go, ladies!" Luna stepped forward and then looked back while the rest of us stood there. "What?"

"I mean…is it necessary or even smart, really, to just dive into the middle of this? We'd better take our time," Miss Elva said, crossing her arms over her sequins and leaning back against the front of the Land Rover as she surveyed the muscular half-naked men racing about.

"It wouldn't be prudent, no," my mother agreed.

"Mom! Seriously." I shook my head, but you didn't see me marching forward either.

"I think just a few more minutes, okay? It will give us a chance to really figure out what is going on." Miss Elva and Abigail both tilted their heads sideways as a fireman in his boxer briefs bent over to look under a truck.

"Abigail! You are a married woman!" Luna laughed.

"I can still look at the menu, honey. I just don't have to order anything."

"I can't…" I shook my head and turned back to where

a few more men ran through the firehouse. I mean, they were certainly fit, I had to give them that. I suppose all that running up and down ladders and whatnot was good for the physique.

"Ladies!" Luna snapped her fingers in front of us. "Control your ovaries."

"Oh, trust me, I am," Miss Elva smiled widely at a large man who glanced over at her. "I really am."

"Are you still dating the Flamingo King? You're driving the car he gave you." Luna pointed to the flamingo-pink Land Rover.

"We have an open relationship, darling. I'm not on a diet like Abigail here."

Luna turned to me and gave me a look like she would burn my side of the shop down if I didn't herd these two into taking care of business.

"That's it. Both of you are embarrassing yourselves. Buy a fireman calendar and ogle them from afar like the rest of us. Plus, who wants to see their fantasy guy running from a magickal tiny man beast thing? It doesn't do much for their appeal, right?"

"Yeah, but it's something they don't understand so that can be scary…" Abigail began and stopped when I glared at her. "Right, right. Yes, best to carry on. Let's catch this bugger."

"Onward, OGs. Onward."

Chapter Sixteen

MISS ELVA SNAGGED the elbow of the burly gentleman she'd been eyeing up.

"Sir, what seems to be the problem here?" Miss Elva's voice went silky smooth, and she batted her eyelashes at the fireman.

"Ma'am. You really shouldn't be here. We've got an unknown threat." The man was all tattoos, muscles, and piercing brown eyes. I think more than one of us drooled.

"Oh my. That sounds dangerous. Perhaps I can help you with your threat?" Miss Elva reached out and trailed a finger down his chest.

"She did not just do that," I whispered to Luna, in awe of Miss Elva's boldness.

"It appears that she did. She really really did." Luna shook her head and tugged me forward, but not before I heard Miss Elva ask what the size of the threat was.

"She's lost her damn mind. How she can flirt in the middle of this?" I held my hands up and jumped as a horn blared. Clapping my hands over my ears, I glared toward the fire truck.

"He's in the truck!" Luna cried. Or at least that's what I thought she said as my ears were still ringing from the blast of the horn. It felt like I'd stood too close to the speaker at a rock concert. Following Luna, I kept my hands over my ears protectively just in case the little shit decided to try it again. When we reached the truck, Luna hauled herself up to the cab, and then turned to shake her head at me.

"Gone."

A horn blasted from another truck and I jumped.

"Can you do a silencing spell or something?" I called to Luna.

"Miss Elva! *Sparkles*!" Luna yelled and Miss Elva turned from her flirtations to look at us. "The noise?"

"Oh, sure thing, honey," Miss Elva called as she dug in her bottomless tote. Pulling something out, she tossed a small pouch across the floor and mouthed some words. In moments, the horns and the sirens had dimmed. They hadn't stopped, but it was as though we'd all put headphones on and now the sounds were muffled background. The firemen looked up confused. Now, they turned and eyed us warily.

"What's going on here?" Miss Elva's man stepped forward and assessed us. "Are you the ones causing all this funny stuff?"

"Nope, we're trying to stop it, sugar," Miss Elva smiled up at him.

"I swear I saw like a little…it had to have been a little

person?" He scratched his head in confusion. "But like… smaller than even a little person. I'm not sure."

"You did. They're called sprites. They live in the other realm but pop over to wreak havoc on ours when they get invited in," Miss Elva supplied helpfully.

"A sprite? I've never heard of such a thing."

"I'd be happy to tell you more. Over drinks one night? Say next week?" Miss Elva smiled up at him and my mouth fell open when he nodded.

"I'd like that."

"Here's my card. Call me. Well, don't. I don't like phone calls. Text me." Miss Elva handed him a card that was covered in glitter and I almost rolled my eyes, thinking about how long it would take to get that glitter off his hands. He apparently didn't mind as he gave Miss Elva a wide smile and a wink.

"One would think we're on a dating show and not trying to catch a manic deity that has been set loose on Tequila Key," I said to Luna.

"It's astounding, really."

"And that, ladies, is how it's done." Miss Elva swaggered over to us. Were we back to the cowboy walk? She was doing a lot of swaggering these days.

"Well done, you. A most excellent choice," Abigail beamed at Miss Elva like she was a child who picked the right answer in a quiz.

"Can we please focus? I'd like to get home and to my bed at some point today." I wasn't exactly whining, but I could feel it coming on.

"He's over here!" A shout sounded from someone at the back of the station.

"Get 'em, ladies!" Abigail shot past me and we followed her, pushing past startled firemen, and came to the back where one man pointed to an open doorway leading to a kitchen. We all crowded into the doorway and peered gingerly inside.

The sprite lounged in front of the fridge, just finishing off a bottle of Miller Lite. When he saw us, he burped and threw the beer bottle lightning fast. It shattered at our feet, spraying shards of glass, and we all jumped back. A manic laugh came from the back.

"That little…" Miss Elva reached in her purse and threw something into the kitchen before anyone could react.

When a flash and a loud boom sounded, we all jumped further back, and Luna grabbed Miss Elva's arm before she dug something else out of her bag.

"Stop! You can't just throw random spells at it. You'll likely make him stronger if he absorbs your magick!" Luna exclaimed.

"Oops." Miss Elva's eyes grew wide as alarms went off, and we all screamed when the overhead sprinklers shot on, exploding water over everything.

"My Chanel!" My mother tucked her purse under her t-shirt.

"My sequins!" Miss Elva shrieked.

"My…" Oh hell. I realized I wasn't wearing anything expensive, and I certainly hadn't done my makeup for this particular excursion. Let the water come – I could do with a shower anyway.

"He's gone. The back window is shattered." Luna, looking like a golden mermaid with her hair plastered to her head, came out of the kitchen. Men raced past us to check the danger and shortly the sprinklers were turned off. As one, we turned and surveyed the mess.

The kitchen was close to destroyed – at the least the refrigerator was. Miss Elva had managed to blow the contents clear across the room and now everybody's leftovers were currently sliding down the cabinets. The firemen slowly gathered in a semi-circle around us, half-naked and dripping wet, their expressions surly.

"Care to elaborate about what happened here?" A fireman stepped forward and crossed his arms over his chest.

"Nope, we most certainly don't," Abigail smiled at everyone. "It's a matter of national security. Pretend you saw nothing."

"I know *I* won't pretend I saw nothing." Miss Elva leered at the men, winking at the one who she had a drinks date with next week.

A throat cleared behind the group and we turned to see Chief Thomas shaking his head at us.

"Ladies? A word?" Chief Thomas asked.

"Chief – they're going to have to pay for this," one man said.

"Yeah, that was my momma's lasagna," another man complained.

"We will get to that. I've worked with these ladies before, and I can assure you that they weren't deliberate in their destruction. It just sort of…seems to happen." Chief Thomas pinched the bridge of his nose.

"In all fairness, most of the times the trouble finds us,"

I pointed out and he shot me a look that seemed to say *be quiet*. "What? I'm just saying."

"Say less of it," Chief Thomas suggested and I closed my mouth.

"Call me." Miss Elva blew a kiss to the hottie and he grinned at her.

Slowly, we followed Chief Thomas out of the firehouse and into the parking lot where a few bystanders had gathered.

"Nothing to see here, folks. It was just a glitch in the security system. They've got it all patched up now." Chief Thomas answered a few questions and waited until people walked away before turning to us. "Out with it."

"Do you know what a sprite is?" Luna asked. I stared at her suspiciously. How was her hair already dry? And her clothes were barely wrinkled. The rest of us were still soaked. One of these days I was just going to sit on her until she gave up her spell for her glamor magick. I knew she used one – there was no possible way she could be this put together after the dousing we just took.

"I'm assuming you're not talking about the soda-pop?"

"No, sir. We're not."

"Another one of those magickal creatures of yours?"

"I mean…he's not ours. We're just trying to find him," I offered.

"What, exactly, is a sprite?" Chief Thomas asked, his voice tense.

"Um, well, he's about this tall." Abigail held her hands about a foot apart. "Little guy. Not really fully in this world. He can bounce between this realm and others.

Magick, of course. Kind of like a fairy but not a fairy exactly. Loves to find trouble. He likes chaos. They thrive on the quicksilver emotions of humans. They like extremes. Big anger. Big laughter. Fun, dance, party. Fight. Explosions. Destruction. Happy or sad, they don't really care. It's all entertainment to them, you see? So, we naturally would like to catch this wee beastie before he destroys the town."

"And you are?" Chief Thomas cocked his head at my mother.

I realized Chief Thomas hadn't met my mother yet and quickly made introductions. He looked from me to her, and I just shrugged and smiled.

"I can see the resemblance," Chief Thomas said and I was surprised. Not everyone would see the similarities between my mother and me, as she had much more polish than I did.

"She's the best part of me," Abigail said and slid an arm around my shoulder. I swear if we weren't standing in the middle of a mess, I would have cried right then and there.

"I don't think I really like what you're saying about this spritey thing destroying the town. No, ladies, I most certainly do not." Chief Thomas shook his head and then squinted at our shirts. "Is that a uterus? What in the world? What does OG stand for?"

"Ovary Gang," Miss Elva smiled brightly at him. "Take 'em down."

"Take who down?" Chief Thomas demanded.

"Oh, that's just a slogan we're trying out. You got any better ideas?"

"I'm screwed," Chief Thomas muttered and pinched his nose again.

"Hmm, that has a ring to it. But I'm not sure that's totally what we're going for," Miss Elva said and then shut her mouth when Chief Thomas glared at her.

"How do we find this thing? And disarm it?"

"Well, that's the tricky bit." Luna walked to Chief Thomas and patted his arm. "It's going to be worse before it gets better. Basically, we have to follow his path of destruction and then manage to subdue and contain him. He's fast though, so we need to somehow distract him long enough that we can work our magick."

"And what, exactly does that entail?" Chief Thomas asked.

"I don't know yet. I'm sorry," Luna said.

"Great. Just great. And this all happened...how?"

"Edna Lewis," Miss Elva said, throwing Edna neatly under the bus. "Edna Lewis, she lives on Coral Ridge Lane. She started all this. I'm sure you should make her responsible for the damages."

"Let's just catch the spritey. Then I'll deal with the lot of you." Chief Thomas looked at us as we all stood there. "Well? Let's go? Get in the car."

"Right, are we riding with you?" I eyed the cruiser.

"Abigail. Will you join me in the cruiser? Luna?"

"Looks like it's just us again, Popcorn," Miss Elva whispered to me.

I got behind the wheel of the pink Land Rover. "Let's ride, Sparkles."

Chapter Seventeen

WE FOLLOWED the police cruiser at a sedate pace, slowly driving the streets with the windows down and listening for any other chaos that might be erupting. The night was peaceful, with clear skies and a light wind, and I suddenly craved sitting on my back porch with my dog and Trace and just...being. Just existing quietly with the person I cared about. I hadn't had a moment to even be with Trace since we'd decided to get back into a relationship this morning, and I wished our timing had been better. I should have been with him, instead of out chasing down weird goblin leprechaun fairy beasts.

"What's with the sigh?" Miss Elva asked.

"Ah, well." I slid a glance at her, wondering if I would annoy her with my relationship talk. Miss Elva was always so decisive about the men she chose to be with and here I'd waffled back and forth between two men for ages. "Trace and I had a nice time this morning."

"I hope by nice time you mean between the sheets?"

"No, silly. We went for a dive together. The first one in a long time. And…we talked."

"I hope that talking leads to more between-the-sheets time. You could use some relaxation."

"Excuse me? I *am* relaxed!" My voice pitched higher, and Miss Elva shot me a knowing look.

"Anywhoooo…" I glared at her. "We decided to get back together."

I waited for her to give me a hard time or to lecture me about my wishy-washy ways. Instead, I was surprised to see a smile spread across her face.

"For real this time? None of that back-and-forth nonsense?" Miss Elva asked.

"For real this time. He made it clear that if I pulled away again, we'd be done. He said his heart can't handle it."

"Smart man. I've wanted this for you, Althea."

"You have?" I looked at Miss Elva – supporter of free love and multiple bed partners – with surprise. "I thought you wanted me to jump on every man available."

"Only if your heart wasn't taken. But it is. You gave it to Trace a while back. You just took some time realizing that."

"Huh." I sat back against the seat and we rode in silence for a bit before I spoke again. "I guess I didn't realize what I needed. I'm having a lot of epiphanies this week."

"That's how it works sometimes. You just roll along until you get slapped in the face and the universe forces you to make some decisions."

"Like you slapping Edna earlier?" I laughed.

"Psh, that was barely a tap. She's always been dramatic. I'm happy for you, Althea. You and Trace fit together in a way that makes sense and it's been a real trial for me to keep my mouth shut about what you should do with your love life."

I bit my tongue because I was fairly certain there wasn't much Miss Elva kept to herself. I glanced over as she picked up her iPhone and scrolled through it for a moment.

"Are you texting Luna?"

"Nope, just cuing up the music for the next part."

"What next…" I jumped as Chief Thomas hit the sirens, the lights on his cruiser flashing red and blue, and floored the cruiser down the street. When music blared through the car, I jumped again.

"Woooo, boyo! Take 'em down!" Miss Elva crowed and slapped the dashboard as the song "Bad Boys" blasted through the speakers.

"You've got to be kidding me," I muttered as I hit the accelerator and raced the Land Rover after the police cruiser.

"Don't act like you don't know this song. Everyone knows this song. It's catchy." Miss Elva rocked her shoulders to the beat, bobbing her head, her sequins shimmering. Despite my fears that I would run us off the road trying to keep up with Chief Thomas, I began to sing.

She wasn't wrong – it *was* a catchy song. There was something about it that fired me up so that when we screeched to a stop behind the police cruiser, where everyone had already gotten out and was looking horrified at the Land Rover, I tumbled out of the car with an attitude.

"Take 'em down!" I shouted.

"That's enough of that," Chief Thomas ordered and I hunched my shoulders.

"Right, sorry. I got carried away." I shrugged an apology to Luna, whose eyes were crinkling with laughter.

A scream immediately sobered me. Turning, we raced up the sidewalk – Chief Thomas in the lead with his gun drawn – and turned toward a row of hedges to see a woman behind them in a long white nightgown with her hands to her mouth.

"Ugh. We were just here last week," Miss Elva complained.

Once again, we'd found ourselves on Theodore Whittier's lawn in the middle of the night, trying to save his sorry ass from trouble. Was I bitter about Theodore? Yeah, I guess I was. He'd tried enough times to discredit me and my business. But perhaps as part of this new growth thing that I was leaning into, I should try and take another tactic with him. Instead of letting him annoy me, I was just going to pity him instead, I decided, as I studied his fancy house and what was once perfectly manicured gardens before zombies had destroyed the bushes the week prior. This wasn't a life that I craved for myself and I knew that Theodore expended a lot of effort on keeping up pretenses. It had to be exhausting to try to be perfect all the time. In the end, nobody really was. So, why bother?

"Is he…" Luna tilted her head as we caught sight of the sprite dancing across the porch.

"You put that little pecker away, Mister!" Miss Elva

shouted, startling the sprite from where he was flashing a distraught Mrs. Whittier. "It's nothing to be proud of, that's for sure."

The sprite made a rude gesture in our direction and then zipped inside.

"Well. Isn't he a cheeky little one?" Abigail asked and then paused when Luna grabbed her arm. "What?"

"It's best we approach this house slowly," Luna said. After last week's debacle where Theodore clearly had no idea how to use his shotgun, we'd learned it was smartest not to go running into the house. Luna advised Chief Thomas of the same, who nodded quietly, and motioned for us to stay behind him. Together we slowly approached the sobbing Mrs. Whittier.

"Ma'am. Are you okay?" Chief Thomas asked quietly.

"I most certainly am not! That...thing...it's disgusting!" Eyes wet with tears, Mrs. Whittier glared indignantly at us. "He...he..."

"Yes, we saw. Not much he should brag about, in my opinion. Even for a little man, you'd think he'd be better proportioned. Maybe that's why he's so full of fury. Little man syndrome, you know?" Miss Elva held up her fingers an inch apart and nodded sagely. Mrs. Whittier's mouth gaped open like a fish gasping for air, completely unable to fathom how to address Miss Elva's comments.

"Why don't you come with me and we'll wait in the car?" Abigail stepped forward and wrapped an arm around Mrs. Whittier, guiding her down the steps.

"But...but...Theo..." Mrs. Whittier turned her head to look back at the house.

"He'll be just fine. There's an officer of the law on the scene now. Well, now, don't you just have the loveliest gardens. Are those begonias?" Abigail expertly distracted Mrs. Whittier as they left the house and I turned back to see what Chief Thomas would do next.

A window shattered as something flew through the glass and landed at our feet. I took a moment to marvel at why this fancy house didn't have double-paned glass or something stronger before I realized what was at my feet.

"Is that a bust of Julius Caesar?" Luna asked carefully.

"With a ball-gag in its mouth?" Miss Elva made a tsking noise with her mouth. "Naughty, naughty, Theodore. Who knew you were such a bad boy? I was certain you weren't the sex dungeon type."

"I can't…I just can't anymore…" I widened my eyes at Luna and silently begged her to make it stop. I wasn't sure just how much more I could take of *any* of the images that I had been subjected to this evening, really.

"Well, the sprite has a sense of humor at least." Luna shrugged as we crept closer. Slowly, we climbed the wooden stairs until we were standing by the large front door that was hanging open. We all peered in the hallway just in time to see Theodore lumber down the hallway – his bathrobe hanging open to show a huge white sagging belly and loose tightie-whities – and an AR-15 clutched in his hands.

My heart, quite simply, froze.

I'd thought last week's run in with Theodore and a shotgun was terrifying, but…this? When had he even had time to acquire a gun like that? I'd never seen one in person, and the sheer sight of it was terrifying. Distinctly at odds with the fancy oriental rug in the hallway and the crystal chandelier, the gun stood out like a wolf sleeping among lambs.

Chief Thomas swore under his breath. "Do. Not. Enter. This. House."

While I typically wasn't one inclined to follow direct orders, this was something that I could fall in line with – no problem at all.

"Chief. Should you call for back-up? What can we do?" Luna asked, her tone even and direct.

"I need you to stay clear. Call for back-up on the radio. And do not distract me. I can't be worried about keeping you safe, disarming Theodore, and trying to corral a spritey."

Miss Elva opened her mouth but with one look from Luna, shut it again.

"We'll just be out here. Listen…" I patted Chief Thomas's arm. "This isn't worth it. Theodore is only going to hurt himself. The sprite is going to move fast, make loud noises, and he'll be halfway to another spot before you've even gotten to Theodore. There likely isn't going to be much you can do."

"Will bullets stop it?" Chief Thomas asked.

"I'm sorry, but no. Only magick. Save your rounds," Luna said.

Chief Thomas muttered a few choice words and padded silently down the hallway while we all tiptoed off the porch and back out into the garden.

"Should we go around the side? Maybe we'll catch the sprite on the way out?" I asked.

"Might not be a bad idea. But…" Luna looked out to the cars and then back to the garden. The moonlight glowed softly over the manicured lawn, and the silence made the hairs on the back of my neck stand up. It felt like we were sitting ducks.

"Cars. We need to inform Abigail about the weapon." Miss Elva decided, dragging us further from the house. "Plus, if the sprite takes off, we'll be faster on wheels."

"Right." For once, Miss Elva was playing it smart and not reckless, and we all ran for the safety of the cars. I stuck my head in the cruiser window.

"How's it going in here?" I glanced back to where Mrs. Whittier snored lightly, spread out across the back seat. "Did you knock her out?"

"I suggested she might feel better if she got some sleep." My mother smiled sweetly at me.

"Theo's got an AR-15."

"Shit," Mom swore.

"Get in Miss Elva's car. We're going to chase the sprite if he gets flushed out. Don't go near the house."

"You couldn't pay me to. Nothing good will come of that situation."

We all climbed into Miss Elva's car, my mother back at the wheel, and she turned the car on to idle while we waited. Nobody spoke.

Rapid gunfire broke out and we all gasped at once.

Chief Thomas and Theodore came racing from the house and jumped in the police cruiser. Chief Thomas turned to make sure we were all in our car before speeding off down the street.

"I think that's our cue to go…" I whispered as more shots split the night.

"I'm afraid to pull forward past the house," Abigail said.

"Just reverse down the street a bit. We'll still be able to see but won't be as close." Luna urged.

Abigail did as instructed, her red hair sticking out wildly from her head, her hat long gone, and soon we were parked further down the block. Theodore's mansion blazed with light and I cringed as it sounded like every window in the house shattered. Rapid gunfire continued, with explosions and glass breaking, until all the dogs in the neighborhood had started barking. Lights began to switch on down the block and I was worried a neighbor would come out and potentially get hurt.

"What do we do?"

"There he is!" Miss Elva shouted. The sprite had danced out onto the street. Seeing our car, he pounded his chest like an ape, let out a little war cry, and streaked down the street. "Follow that imp!"

I jerked back in my seat as my mother hit the accelerator, and the car sped after the sprite.

"At least he didn't bring the gun," I said, having caught a glance of Theodore's destroyed mansion.

"Must have run out of ammo," Miss Elva shrugged. "Theodore's gonna have a hell of a time cleaning that up."

The car filled with silence. I know I should have felt bad – I know it – but somehow, I couldn't bring myself to do so. When a snicker escaped, I pressed my lips together and looked out the window.

"Damn shame about that bust of Caesar," Miss Elva said.

And with that, I lost it and all my pent-up nerves dissolved into hysterical laughter. I mean, if I didn't laugh I'd cry, right?

Chapter Eighteen

WE CHASED the sprite down to the water where he promptly leapt into the ocean and disappeared into the dark depths.

"What can I do?" I cried, thinking about my newly discovered Sea Witch powers.

"Nothing. If you don't already have a containment spell in place, once he hits the water, he'll have bounced through into another realm to have a nap before recharging for another day of fun."

"So...that's it?" I asked. "There's nothing else we can do?"

"We get some sleep, Althea. That way we'll be recharged for whatever we deal with tomorrow," Luna said.

"But...how do we even know he'll come back here? Why not like reappear in Las Vegas or something?" I asked. "Wouldn't that be much more enticing for him?"

"He's tied here. The spell that brought him keeps him tied in a fairly small radius. The further he goes from his entry point or birthplace, I guess, the more his power weakens. If he stays here, he'll be at his strongest. Trust me, he'll find plenty to have fun with here." Luna sighed, and checked a message on her phone. "I'm ready for bed. Can we agree to pick this up tomorrow?"

"Yes. I'll set a spell when I get home," Miss Elva said. "I'll just blanket the city. I'll get a warning when he re-enters our realm."

"Can you do that?" I squinted at Miss Elva. Truly, the depth of her knowledge was insane.

"Of course, honey. There isn't much Miss Elva can't do. You know that." Miss Elva patted her hat.

"That's a mighty handy spell," I said to her. "I feel like we'll be able to sleep peacefully, at least."

"Unless he chooses to come back real early. Then the OG gang has to ride deep," Miss Elva said.

"It's unlikely. Sprites expend an exorbitant amount of energy when they are in this realm. He'll need to rest," Luna said.

"What about the shop tomorrow?" I asked Luna.

"We'll close. Can you cancel your clients?" Luna glanced back at me and I nodded. It wasn't a practice I preferred to do, but generally speaking that just meant I would be working on a Saturday instead.

We dropped Luna at her sleek condo before returning to my house. Miss Elva wasted no time hopping behind the wheel and speeding away with "Bad Boys" blaring from her open windows.

"It's three in the morning…" I shook my head as I saw at least one neighbor's light flick on. "Hurry, inside before I get yelled at."

I ushered my mom inside to find a dancing Hank at the door and a snoozing father on the couch.

"He could've gone up to bed..." I said.

"Mitch likes to wait for me. He doesn't like going to bed alone."

"Aww." That was sweet, even if I'd had my limit of thinking about my mother in bed today.

"How'd it go?" My dad blinked, his eyes opening, a smile immediately alighting his face when he saw my mother. "Your hair is a mess, honey."

"Yes, I know. Those dreadful fire sprinklers almost ruined my Chanel." My mother pouted and Dad sat up, patting the spot next to him and she dropped down, curling into his side.

"I'm sorry to hear that. You'll have to tell me all about it. But...maybe tomorrow. It's quite late."

"Does Hank need to go out or anything?" I didn't even want food. I just wanted my bed at this point. But seeing my parents curled together on the couch also made my heart do a funny little twinge. I wanted to talk to Trace, I realized, and tell him about my crazy night. I wanted to curl up with him and fall asleep by his side. Knowing it was too late to bother him though, I went to the kitchen to fill my water bottle before heading toward the stairs, Hank at my heels.

"Trace stopped by." My dad said and I stopped in my tracks.

"He did? What did he want?"

"He wanted to check on you. I think he was worried about this whole sprite situation. You could have explained it better for him." My dad's tone was chastising.

"Did I not? I guess…I don't know. I'm still getting used to sharing those aspects with other people."

"Well, either tell him nothing or give him a good explanation. He was pretty worried about you since you hadn't responded to his text messages."

"Ah, shit. I'd left my phone in my purse in the car. It was pretty hectic." I felt shame wash through me. Day one of being in relationship again and already I was being a bad girlfriend.

My father just shrugged. "Tell that to him. For what it's worth – I like Trace. A lot. He's a good guy, Althea."

"We're back together. We decided it today."

"You are!" My mom sat up and clapped and Hank bounced over to her. He wasn't sure what we were celebrating, but he was always down for a party. "That's fantastic news. This is what I've wanted for you."

"Trace is the one you wanted for me?"

"He's just a really good guy, Althea. Sure, he's got a touch of a wild past. But, who doesn't?" My thoughts flashed to her summer in Europe, and I cringed inside.

"He cares a lot about you," Dad said.

"I care a lot about him. What you said helped me. I'll go…well, I guess give him a text message since it's late." Saying my goodnight, I padded upstairs, exhaustion seeping over me. When I flicked on the light in my room, I almost screamed when I saw Trace snoring in my bed.

"Gah!" I slapped a hand over my mouth and took a few deep breaths. Hank, seeing Trace in bed, took a running leap and landed next to him – waking Trace up.

"Hey buddy," Trace said, and then turned to see me. Much like when my father had looked at my mother – a smile lit Trace's handsome face. He pushed his blond hair back and sat up against the pillow, gathering Hank into his arms. I stood for a moment, just drinking in the sight of him, before closing the door softly behind me.

"Hey, you. I can't believe you're here." I moved forward and stood shyly by the side of the bed.

"Your dad suggested I stay. I felt a little weird coming up to your bed when your parents are here, but he's pretty laid back."

"About as laid back as it gets. Plus, he likes you."

"I like him, too. He's always been good to me. Kind of like a second dad, I guess." We both looked at each other for a moment and then squinched our noses up.

"Maybe let's not do those comparisons? It makes us seem like sister and brother," I suggested.

"Yeah, I got that. Either way, I'm glad I could stay. I've been thinking about you all day. I was worried about this sprite thing you told me about." Trace squinted and leaned forward to look at my shirt. "Is that a uterus?"

"Um, yeah. It is."

"Far out," Trace murmured, and then patted the bed. Dropping down next to him, I leaned in for a loose hug, with Hank smushed between us. I loved that I could show up wearing a t-shirt with ovaries on it and Trace just smiled at me. My father hadn't even blinked when he'd seen us. Trace was definitely my kind of people.

"It's come to my attention that I might need to be a little more in-depth in my explanations of all things magickal to you." I rested a hand on his chest and met his kind eyes. "I'm sorry."

"I don't need to understand it all. But maybe we can

figure out a way where you can check in with me more when you're on one of these missions of yours? I just worry about you is all."

"I...yeah. Bad girlfriend move. Big time. I'm sorry. I didn't even think. Well...that's not true." I leaned over and brushed a kiss over his lips. "I did think about you tonight. I just didn't think to text you because I thought you'd be sleeping, and I'd left my phone in the car. But I did think about you. Quite a bit actually."

"Want to tell me what you were thinking about?" Trace smiled sleepily at me.

"This, actually." I ran my hand down his chest. "Just this. I thought how nice it would be to curl up with you and go to sleep together."

"Let's do it then. I have clients in the morning, so I'll have to be up in a few hours. But I'm glad I'm here. And that you're okay."

"I'm glad you're here, too, Trace. Thanks for staying." I wanted to say that I loved him, but his eyes were already drifting closed. Instead, I slipped my jeans and my bra off, and moved a disgruntled Hank to the foot of the bed so I could slip under the covers with Trace. His arms automatically came around me and I fell instantly to sleep, feeling safe with him by my side.

Chapter Nineteen

I WOKE to an empty bed and blinked at the time on my phone. How was it nine o'clock? I hadn't even noticed Trace leaving, but I did sleep peacefully with him next to me. Stretching, I smiled at where Hank had spread out on the foot of the bed, his little paws pushing against my leg.

I felt good, I realized. Even in the midst of the craziness of last night and the past few weeks – I didn't feel as rattled by stress as I normally would have. Maybe this was what leaning into my power felt like. If so, I needed to embrace these changes more. Luxuriating in a long hot shower, I took my time getting ready before I went downstairs to greet my parents. My father was humming in the kitchen, making scrambled eggs and toast, and my mother was typing away on her laptop.

"Good morning, sweetie. Eggs?" Dad asked, turning from the stove to smile at me. Hank raced to the back door to take care of his morning business, and I walked over to slide the door open and let him out.

"I'd love some, thanks. Did you guys sleep okay?"

"Like a stone. How about you? I heard you had a visitor in your bed?" Mom peered at me over her reading glasses and the fifteen-year-old inside me cringed.

"We just…" I stopped and shook my head. This was my house, and I was an adult, after all. "Yes, Trace was waiting for me. He was worried about my safety last night. I guess I need to be better about checking in with him when I am facing moments of danger."

"Yes, that would be smart. I texted your father, you know."

"Did you? When?"

"A few times. It takes two seconds to shoot off a voice text, Althea. You'll do better next time." Mom went back to her emails and Dad slid me a plate of food. I bellied up to the breakfast counter while Hank skidded back inside, intent on finding his own breakfast. Music played in the background; I enjoyed my breakfast without having to carry on a conversation.

"Any word from Miss Elva?" I asked when I finished.

"Nope. Sprites sleep a while. You'll have some time, I'm sure." My mom continued to type, and I glanced over her shoulder to see her inbox full of messages.

"Damn, Mom. That's a ton of messages."

"And those are just the ones my assistant forwards on to me. I have her filter out a lot."

"I'm going to see if Luna needs help with her online orders since I cancelled my clients for the day."

"Sounds good, honey. We'll stay here with Hank." Dad came over and kissed my forehead. Taking a cup of coffee to go, I biked to the shop, feeling at ease. I found Luna already in the back and she smiled when she saw me.

"You didn't have to come in." Luna looked fresh and lovely in slim white jeans and a pale blue t-shirt with gold stars scattered over it.

"I wanted to help. I'm enjoying this time we're spending together, and it's nice to learn how to mix your tonics. I think it's also making my own magick stronger. I like knowing each ingredient and the properties it has. I think it's helping me to learn more about how to mix and match my own magick, if that makes sense?"

"Of course, it does." Luna smiled at me as she crossed to her worktable with a bundle of lavender in her hand. "It's kind of like learning to cook at your mother's side."

"Or father's side," I said, laughing. "Abigail wasn't much for cooking."

"Or father's." Luna conceded. "So…you and Trace?"

"Yeah, we're back together." I began cutting the lavender as she instructed, the heady scents filling the air around us.

"And you're happy?"

"I am."

"That's all I can ask. I've wanted you to be happy – like I am."

"I haven't seen Mathias in a while. Is he well?" Mathias, Luna's dreamy boyfriend, was an ER doctor and overall amazing human being. I couldn't have picked a more perfect man for her if I'd tried to.

"He is. We're really good, Althea. I think…well, I think we're getting really serious. I mean, I've known for a while it's what I've wanted. And we've talked about it a lot. But it just feels right." Luna beamed at me over her silver mixing bowl and my heart just danced in my chest with happiness for her.

"He'd be an absolute fool not to lock you down. You're the best person I know."

Hours later, we'd gotten Luna up to date on her orders when both of our phones sounded simultaneously with text message notifications.

"The sprite," Luna and I said in unison and grabbed our phones.

"Miss Elva's on the way to pick us up with my mom," I said.

"Let's get everything locked up and be ready out front."

Minutes later, the pink Land Rover skidded to a stop in front of our store with my mother looking terrified in the passenger's seat. As soon as the car stopped, she jumped out and rounded the hood and stood by the driver's side door with her hands on her hips.

"Get out, you crazy banshee."

"Well, someone's ovaries are in a twist this morning." Miss Elva huffed as she pulled herself from the car. She was in pink sparkles today that matched the pink in her OG hat. I was glad I'd brought my hat along, to be honest, because I hadn't bothered to style my hair after my long shower, and it was easy to just tuck into a cap.

"Luna, did you forget your shirt? I have extras!" Miss Elva began to rummage in her purse.

"Great," Luna said, a tight smile on her face. She hopped in the passenger seat again while Miss Elva and I climbed in back. Rosita hovered in the trunk area and I waved my hello to her.

"Okay ladies, I almost didn't call you for this one. But I suppose in the name of good will, I decided to do so," Miss Elva said.

"Why…what's happening?" I glanced at Miss Elva as I pulled my phone from my purse. I had promised myself to try and take my new girlfriend duties seriously, so I was going to text Trace what we were up to.

"The sprite has decided to get himself all fancied up today," Miss Elva chuckled as my mother pulled the Land Rover away from the shop.

"What do you mean?"

"He's currently wrecking Edna's shop," Mom said.

"He is not," I exclaimed, pausing in my texting.

"He is." Miss Elva laughed. "Apparently he has no qualms about destroying the person who brought him here."

"It makes sense. There is a tie to the person who brings you but also there is kind of a love/hate that occurs," Luna mused, running her finger over a page in her Celtic book. "Because his power diminishes the further he travels from here, he'll likely be angry about that."

"It's like a kid lashing out at their parents," Abigail added.

"A little bit. Except Edna really doesn't control what the sprite does. It's just the nature of the spell that his power will diminish as he moves away from his birthplace, so to speak. I mean, it's weird. It's not like he was birthed here. He existed before this. It's just where he was brought through. His landing place?" Luna asked.

"Dare I say that Edna's place is his uterus?" I asked.

Silence filled the car for a moment before a whoop from Miss Elva made us all crack up.

"Oh, I like that, honey. I really like that. I mean, it's more like Edna was the delivery canal if you get what I'm saying, but it's real funny to me." Miss Elva laughed. I was laughing as I finished texting Trace, letting him know where I was and what problems might occur. He was on the dive boat for the day, but when he got back within range of land, his cell phone would ping through with my text.

"Luna, I've been thinking about something and have a question for you." Abigail looked over at Luna who glanced up from her Celtic book.

"Of course, what can I help with?"

"Well, you know I have a clientele list that's a mile long. And my customers are very well off."

"Yes, they certainly are," Luna agreed.

"I have been toying with developing a relaxation line. One of the biggest complaints my clients come to me with is anxiety. Worry for the future. Being unable to sleep. I'm thinking about developing specific tonics or teas that will help in those areas," Abigail said.

"I like the idea and would be happy to help. It's such a needless thing, isn't it? This worry for the future? I know it's hardwired into us as humans, but just think how much happier people would be if they focused on what they could control in the next hour – the next day, even? So much of that strain would go away because they could chip away at their bigger worries if they broke it down into incremental chunks."

We all looked at Luna like she'd just sprouted two heads.

"Well, now, that's positively insightful, Luna. You should be giving one of those Ted talks. I'd watch it," Miss Elva observed.

"Thanks," Luna's cheeks flushed.

"Does that mean you'll be staying around for a while, Mom?" I asked.

"I think so, honey. At least to work on this project. Would you mind terribly if we were in your hair for a bit?"

"Not in the slightest. I've loved having you here." Happiness flooded me that my little family would be together for a while longer yet.

"Abigail. Speaking of those fancy clients of yours…" Miss Elva turned. "Have I mentioned that I'm about to launch my own fashion line? I have to imagine many of my luxury caftans would appeal to that particular clientele."

"Oh, I was already on your website this morning. I pre-ordered another white one with the crystal turquoise beading on the trim. It's going to go perfectly against my red hair. I'll proudly share your collection, Elva. My clients love finding up-and-coming designers. They like to feel like they've discovered something that nobody else has. You'll be a hit; I can promise you that."

"Up-and-coming designer," Miss Elva laughed and struck a pose. "Do you hear how fancy I am, everyone? I'll expect you to treat me accordingly."

"We already treat you like a princess," I said.

"I think she wants to be queen," Rosita piped up from the back.

"Well, then Queen Elva it is." Abigail laughed.

"Hey," I leaned forward and tapped Luna's shoulder. "Can you give us any tips on what to do when we see the sprite? I feel like we can just spend hours running after him, and I'm not sure what to *actually* do."

"I think that I can. It isn't just one spell to get rid of him though. First, we need a containment spell. Then we need a transportation spell that takes him home. The tricky part is he uses water to transport. So, let's say we contain him at Edna's shop – well, we still need to get him to a spot to transport."

"Can it be like a cup of water?" Miss Elva asked.

"Unfortunately, no. Natural. Ocean, rivers, lakes."

"So, basically we need to either contain him and move him to the water. Or we need to lure him to a spot by the water and hit him with a transport spell."

"I don't know any containment spells." Anxiety trickled low in my stomach.

"Right now, it's too late to learn. Remember one thing, Althea." Luna turned and met my eyes. "Intention is everything in magick."

"Okay." We pulled to a stop in front of a pretty red brick building with a black awning and large glass windows showcasing wedding gowns. I gasped as one of the wedding gowns got ripped from a mannequin and disappeared into the shop.

"Edna's gonna lose her shit," Miss Elva said. We all sat still for a moment, watching as another gown went sailing across the room.

"We should really go in," Abigail said.

"It would be the right thing to do," I agreed.

Nobody moved.

"Ladies! That's enough. The OG gang does not sit around and let a sprite terrorize our town. Let's take 'em down!" Luna ordered in a fierce tone and we all jumped into action.

Edna had better thank us later, I thought.

Chapter Twenty

I DUCKED as a floral crown sailed at my head from across the room.

"Hey!" I shouted.

Manic laughter drifted at me from a different direction than from where the crown had come from.

Under normal circumstances, the shop seemed like it would have been a lovely spot to try bridal gowns on. The walls were painted a dove gray and there was gold detailing on the crown molding. The main room held several racks of dresses, a wall of mirrors, and several mannequins sporting different styles. Through a double doorway to the back, there were several fitting areas each with a changing room, a pedestal to stand on, and a floor length mirror.

At the moment, however, it was an explosion of lace and tulle. Dresses had been thrown off the racks, bolts of fabric unwound, and ribbons lay in heaps on the floor. Edna screeched from the fitting area, where she was ducking down and trying to avoid...were those seamstress pins he was darting at her?

"That's enough!" Luna ordered and the sprite dropped the pins, turning to leer at us. In a blur of movement, he zipped to the other side of the shop and I saw a bundle of dresses moving.

In seconds, a dress stood up from the floor as if of its own accord and began to parade around the room. The sprite popped his head through the neckline and put his arms out as though he were posing on a runway. The dress was a strapless white ballgown style with a beaded sweetheart neckline and the sprite clutched the dress to his bosom as he sashayed across the floor.

"Oh, I like his style," Miss Elva called. "Yes, honey. Sashay all day! Work it. Work it."

The sprite, loving the encouragement, jerked his shoulders and began a runway walk around the room, the dress floating behind him. How he managed to walk essentially on air while holding up that heavy dress was beyond me, but despite my misgivings, my lips quirked into a smile. I had to say, the little man was owning that dress. He twirled at the end and struck a pose.

"Not bad, little guy. I'd give you a seven out of ten." Miss Elva clapped, and the sprite's face went furious. He dropped the dress and argued incomprehensibly at Miss Elva, his little fists in the air.

"Well, don't get mad at me. It wasn't the right dress for you is all. Here...what about the one with the sequins? I do love a good sparkle."

The sprite turned and looked at the dress that Miss Elva pointed at. In the meantime, I saw Luna hurriedly paging through her Celtic book, her head bent next to my mother's. Turning back, I saw that the sprite had eschewed Miss Elva's choice, instead picking up a mermaid style dress in blush pink that ended with tulle roses at the hem.

"Hmm, let's see it. I think the color could be good for you." Miss Elva tapped a finger against her mouth and the sprite made the dress stand up to its full height and then disappeared inside before popping his head out of the top. Turning, he somehow made the dress do a slinky walk around the room in a slow seductive circle. The sprite turned, throwing us a look over his shoulder, and then continued sauntering. When his back was turning, Miss Elva glanced at Luna who motioned for her to continue.

"I think that's just the ticket, honey. As I thought, that's a great color for you. What are you going to wear underneath?"

The sprite paused, tilting his head as he considered it. Dropping the dress to the floor, he bounced over to what looked to be a rack of undergarments. I ducked as a garter flew towards me, followed by a corset. The pile of fabrics shifted and moved until the sprite emerged with what must have once been a lace thong wrapped around him like a corset. He'd improvised, and I couldn't fault his attempt at design.

"That's just perfect. It really is. Now…for a headpiece? I'm thinking maybe just a touch of sparkle because you already have all the pow with the color in the dress." Miss Elva held up a small comb with a sparkly flower at the end of it. The sprite glared at her and stomped his foot.

"Okay, honey. Okay. I know a bridezilla when I see one. You want a crown, don't you?"

The sprite nodded, crossing his arms over his chest.

"No problem. Look – there's a whole rack over here. You can do a sparkly tiara. Or a floral one. Or just a touch of sparkle. Even just a gold circlet."

The sprite turned and walked over to examine the rack and Miss Elva stepped back, giving Luna and my mother ample space to cast their spell.

Stepping forward, the women chanted quietly together and then threw their hands out, pushing a wave of magick to the sprite.

In that same instant, Edna surged forward, rage contorting her features as she leapt to capture the sprite. The spell hit her full force and she dropped to the floor with a thud. The sprite jumped, turning to examine Edna's prone form on the floor.

"She just tripped," Miss Elva said smoothly. "She's not used to gowns on the floor like this. Clumsy of her." The sprite looked between the two, his eyes narrowed, before returning to his crown selection.

"I'll just check on Edna." I announced. I didn't want the sprite to think I was going to jump him, though it was tempting having him stand still long enough. Kneeling by Edna's body, I turned her body gently to the side.

Her eyes blinked at me, but it seemed like she couldn't move. At the very least, she was breathing, so that was something I supposed.

As a little squeal rang out, I glance up to see the sprite had chosen a sparkly crown and was dancing his way toward the door. I didn't think we'd have much longer with him.

"Luna," I whispered.

"Say, Althea – when is that big party you're having tonight?" Miss Elva asked loudly.

"What…" I started to ask when Miss Elva glared at me with a look that said, *I will eat your firstborn if you speak another word.*

"Yeah, your happy hour at the beach tonight? I want to invite that hot firefighter. He called me last night. I told him about the huge party you were going to have. Music. Drinks. Dancing. Fireworks. All right by the water. It's going to be insane, right?"

"Right," I said. Had she lost her damn mind?

"Probably the biggest party Tequila Key's ever seen. I don't know how anyone would miss out on such fun."

I could see the sprite had stopped by the broken front window, his head cocked toward Miss Elva.

"What's your address again honey? 5 Surfside Lane? I'll just text it to him."

"Yes. That's the correct address. It's at happy hour tonight. It's going to be *so* much fun," Luna said.

"I can't decide what to wear. Maybe my blue sequins?" Miss Elva asked me, never looking toward the sprite.

"Definitely sparkles. You look your best in them," I agreed.

"He's gone," Mom said, and I looked at Miss Elva in confusion.

"Sprites love a big party. Like…*love* them. Half the time the reason they are creating destruction is that they have all this pent-up energy and want to use it somewhere. They just want to drink and dance and all that. If we had a good club in Tequila Key, he would have been up all night raving. Trust me, they go mental in New York City."

"I'm sorry. I didn't have enough time to run a second containment spell. He was already suspicious after Edna fell." Luna came forward, her pretty face twisted in concern.

"It's okay, child. We do the best we can. 'Sho we do. No way for you to suspect this old hag right here would interfere with your spell." Miss Elva nudged Edna with her foot. Edna's mouth worked, but no sound came out.

"That was smart of you, Elva. Though I'd better call Mitchell to warn him in case the sprite shows up early."

"Have him go to Trace's. Or to Lucky's. Just get him and Hank off the property," I called to my mother as she stepped out the front door.

"Don't worry about Hank." Luna looked up at me from where she crouched by Edna's head. "Despite the chaotic nature of a sprite, they are in tune with the natural world. They won't hurt animals."

"That makes me feel somewhat better."

"Can you help me lift her?" Luna asked and I went to kneel by Edna's body. Together, we lifted her bony frame and moved her to a little couch in the back of the shop. Once there, we propped her up on some cushions. Edna's beady eyes tracked us, but otherwise she was unable to move.

"Is this your containment spell then?" I asked, studying Edna with my hands on my hips.

"Yes. It's like invisible rope wrapped all around the body. If we had gotten the sprite, we could've just taken him to the water and then done our transport spell."

"You hear that Edna?" Miss Elva came and put her hands on her hips. "Once again, you screwed something up. If you had just let us do our magick, we would have taken care of him."

Edna's eyes narrowed and I decided to refrain from pointing out that Miss Elva had also interfered with a spell. Not to say that Edna's spell would have actually called down a goddess, but still – here we were.

"Are goddesses tricky to deal with?" I asked, my curiosity piqued.

"Oh, my. Yes, they are impossible." Luna laughed. "It's important they stay where they are – ruling from afar. Having a goddess around is like trying to tell Miss Elva to tone it down."

I looked at Miss Elva who had launched into a full-on lecture for Edna. Her sequins sparkled in the track lighting above and her attitude was on point. No, there was no filtering Miss Elva.

"I'm assuming you can't tell a goddess what to do."

"Nope. I'm actually quite thankful we're only dealing with a sprite. A goddess, well, we'd have to call in the big guns."

Before I could ask what the big guns were, Luna blew a wave of magick at Edna and the containment spell must have evaporated because she slumped suddenly on the couch and then pushed herself shakily up.

"Oh, shut it, you cow," Edna said and Miss Elva stepped forward.

"Stop!" Mom cried, having come back inside. Pushing through us, she took a seat next to Edna who was shaking as she moved her limbs again. Crossing her legs gracefully, Abigail tilted her head at Edna. "Edna?"

"Yes?" Edna looked suspiciously at my mother.

"This has to stop."

"I…"

"Just listen for a moment. Elva, quiet." Abigail ordered and Miss Elva glared at her, but stopped whatever she was about to say. "I'm sorry about your shop. It looks like you have some really lovely things here, and I know this place is really important to you."

I was shocked to see tears fill Edna's eyes as she looked around her shop in abject despair.

"We're going to stay here and help you put this to rights the best we can."

"We are?" Miss Elva put a hand on her hip.

"We are." Abigail glared at Miss Elva. "Because I think Edna needs to learn a little about what it means for women to stick together. And it's time we had a serious talk about her magick."

"You'd really help me?" Edna shuddered a breath in.

"Of course." We all nodded, well Luna and I did. Miss Elva seemed to be examining a loose thread on her top.

"I'd appreciate that," Edna finally said.

"First, though. It's time to really talk about what you're trying to accomplish with the Seven Star Sister Society. You've been going at this for years, but to what purpose? From my estimation, it seems like you cause more harm than good. What's going on here? Why are you making your life more difficult? Help me to understand, Edna. No, don't get all defensive on me." Abigail wrapped an arm around Edna's shoulders which had gone stiff. "I'm honestly trying to understand."

"Well…" Edna sighed and twisted her hands in her lap. "I…I guess it's just that there was a part of me that always wanted to be something more. To have something more. Power. Magick. My mother, you see, she was a great ballerina. I'm not sure if you knew that?" Edna glanced at us and then pointed to where a picture of a woman dressed for Swan Lake stood en pointe hung on the wall.

"She's lovely," I said, crossing to study the photo.

"I never really got much time with her, you see? She was always traveling. She wore the most majestic costumes and all but flew through the air. Her talent was world-renowned. I was convinced, from a young age, that she was magick. And, well, I was an after-thought in her world." Edna's shoulder's slumped and my mother's eyes met mine with a questioning look. I knew what she was asking me – had I felt the same way with her traveling? Smiling, I shook my head no, and she turned back to Edna.

"I lost her when I was only fifteen. And I guess I've been looking for magick ever since. I found a book around the time that she'd passed on and it talked all about the power of the stars and rituals and...I don't know. Maybe it was a place for me to pour my grief into. I began to practice the spells in earnest and was surprised to see things... happen. As in actually happen. I was making things change out of the power of my own mind and rituals. It was...intoxicating, I suppose. I wanted more. I hungered for more. Somehow, this idea of magick seemed to fill the void where..." Edna stopped speaking and wiped her eyes.

"Where her love should've been," Abigail finished softly for her and squeezed her shoulders.

"Yes, well. It seems I've made a right mess of things," Edna concluded.

"We all make mistakes." Miss Elva stepped forward

and the rest of us looked at her in surprise. "And you do have power, you know. But the problem is you've never looked outside that one book. You latched onto it and thought it was the only way and, unfortunately, it's not the right spell book for you."

"It's not?" Edna looked up at Abigail through her tears.

"It's not. Or you wouldn't constantly be misfiring your magick. Now, I can't be certain because you'll have to learn more, but I suspect you're a craft witch."

"A craft witch?"

"Yes, look around at these gorgeous creations. That *you've* crafted." My mom swept her arm out to the dresses that lay in piles around the room. "This is magick."

"She's right, you know. Coming from my professional expertise," Miss Elva sniffed as she picked up a silk slip dress. "These are real nice, honey."

"You need training. You're not ready to lead – at least not in magicks. Because you're trying to teach your coven the wrong things. I'm sure you've had trouble with them, no?" Abigail asked and Edna nodded slowly.

"Why don't you call them? Invite them over to Althea's for this happy hour party. We'll work together to catch this sprite. After that, we can look at helping everyone find their paths. It will be like one of those soul retreats or something."

"I'd...I'd like that." Edna narrowed her eyes at Miss Elva. "If she doesn't mind, that is."

"I don't mind, Edna. I told you – we all make mistakes. I mean, I'm pretty close to perfect. Like, ninety-nine-point-nine percent perfect. But even I mess up on the rarest of occasions."

I did my best to look anywhere but at Miss Elva.

"Shall we get this cleaned up as best we can before we go to this party I'm supposedly having? Should I go home and get things organized? Pick up drinks? What am I doing?" I asked, looking to Miss Elva.

"Nah, child. He'll be happy if he sees people and music. Remember how much they love to party. We've got people. I've got good music. And knowing you – you've got drinks."

"I mean, a few," I said, feeling a little embarrassed. "It's best to have some if company comes, right?"

"No judgment," Miss Elva held up her hands and turned to pick up a dress. "Now this one here's real nice. You should try this on, Luna."

"Um…" Luna looked taken aback. "We really should clean up."

"Go on, try it on. She's not wrong… it will look lovely on you." Edna sniffed and pointed to a dress rack. "And that one for Althea."

"Wait, what?"

"The lace or the silk?" Miss Elva was already at the rack.

"The lace."

"I am not a lace girl…" I sighed as Miss Elva shoved it in my hands. "Go on."

"Seriously, we have more important things to do."

"What's more important than taking a moment for fun?" Abigail demanded. At her tone, we both slunk into the fitting rooms, grumbling.

"Don't look in the mirror." Miss Elva pushed the curtain open behind me when I was half in the dress.

"Can a woman get some privacy?" I complained, hopping on one foot as I pulled the dress on.

"Nope. You'll need someone to zip you. Turn around." I turned and sighed, letting Miss Elva pull the zipper up. Surprisingly, it closed. I wasn't exactly a bridal sample size.

"This feels nice, actually." Had I gone mad? I wasn't one to really think about marriage or babies or any of that. And here I was saying a bridal gown felt nice?

"Come out," Mom called.

Luna and I both stepped out at the same time and exclaimed over each other. Luna looked stunning in a waterfall of silk that washed over her slim curves like moonlight.

"Luna! You're effervescent!" I exclaimed, feeling tears flood my eyes.

"Althea! I never would have figured you for lace. But you're stunning. Look at yourself," Luna demanded and together we turned toward the mirror.

And, I have to say – she wasn't wrong. I never in a million years would have picked this dress and yet it... well, it worked for me. The soft lace sleeves ended halfway down my arms, and the square cut neckline was surprisingly flattering. The dress fit me through the waist and dropped in soft romantic tiers to the floor. Beneath the white lace tiers was a layer of soft pink, adding some color and dimension to the skirt. I felt like a romantic 1800s heroine, and yet funky and modern, with my dyed curly hair and tattoos.

"Oh, Althea." My mom dabbed her eyes.

"Don't start or we'll all be wailing here in a moment."

I sniffed, dangerously close to tears myself. What was wrong with me?

"Edna, you've got a brilliant eye. Can we make a note of this style – just in case?" Mom asked Edna and she nodded; her own eyes still red from crying.

"Okay, let's do me next."

"Miss Elva!" I turned and laughed at her. "You said you would never get married."

"I know, but I like to try dresses on."

"We should really get going..." Luna began and we noted the stubborn look cross Miss Elva's face.

"Don't you want to design your own dress anyway? A Miss Elva exclusive?" I asked quickly before the storm broke.

"That's true, Althea. That's true. No offense to Edna's handiwork and all, but only I can design the perfect dress for myself."

There was no arguing with that, I decided. Brushing my hands over the lace of the dress once more, I turned and made my way to the fitting room. There'd be time enough for that later.

For now, I had a party to throw.

Chapter Twenty-One

WHEN I ARRIVED at my place, my father had cleared out with Hank, a note on the counter saying he was going to Trace's for some male bonding time.

"What'll they do?" I wondered, holding up the note and looking to my mother.

"Well, your dad doesn't watch sports. Probably grill out and discuss the ingredients of some craft beer?"

"I mean…I guess." Trace was good with customer service, though, and got along with most people. I'm sure they'd muddle their way through. It was kind of cute, actually, picturing them both hanging out. I pulled my phone out, shot another text to Trace, and then dialed a number.

"Who are you calling, Althea?" Luna asked.

"Pizza," I said, and Miss Elva gave me a thumbs-up. I'd missed lunch since we'd been called to Edna's shop and if we were supposed to be having a party – well – we needed to have some food, right? I ordered ten large pizzas, figuring Edna's group would eat some, and if not – well – I'm sure I could give it away somewhere. After that,

I went to where the ladies had pulled two long tables into the backyard and put out plates, cups, and glasses. Little vases held sprigs of greens from my yard, and Miss Elva had switched my fairy lights on. I jumped when music suddenly blared.

"Not rap," Abigail ordered Miss Elva. "We need something more dancey. The sprites like dancing."

"What about like 70s soul? Some disco? Some...Yes Sir, I Can Boogie?"

"I mean...I'm not sure that's soul. But it's dancey. Let's put it on and let the playlist go from there." Miss Elva agreed and soon the two were shimmying across the yard, humming about boogying.

"I mean...it's catchy." Luna smiled at me as I put napkins on the table. Despite myself, I found my hips swaying to the song.

"That's it, Althea!" Miss Elva danced over to me and grabbed my hand. Laughing, I let her swing me out into the yard and soon the four us were dancing in a circle, laughing, as the music swelled around us.

"Ohhhh, I can boogie..." Miss Elva crooned. She had a surprisingly good voice, and we clapped her on as we danced our way across the garden. I looked up as someone called to us. Edna peered at us over the gate to my yard, with the Seven Star Sister Society in line behind her.

"Join us," Abigail cried. And, to my surprise, they did. The women filed in and took zero prodding to hop in the circle and start shaking it. I don't know what Edna had told them after our little talk with her at her shop, but apparently, we were no longer enemies. I was even more delighted when I saw the pizza guy show up and I waved him over to my fence. I'd already paid online, but gave him money for a tip. Dancing back to the table, I put the food down. If I could just get one slice in before that little shit, I mean sprite, showed up, I'd be a happy camper. Reaching in the box, I just clasped my hand around a piece when Miss Elva called out.

"Oh, yeah, there's our little buddy. Shake it little man!"

Damn it. I'd jinxed myself. Sighing, I left the pizza where it was and turned to see the sprite dancing along the edge of the fence. He moved quickly, stopping to shake his hips to the song, and then zipping to another area of the garden.

"Get him a drink. Much like humans, it slows him down." Miss Elva danced her way over, speaking out of the side of her mouth to me. She'd already instructed us at the shop to act like everything was normal even when the sprite showed up. We needed him to sit still in one spot long enough that Luna could contain him and then we could work from there. It appeared the Star Society had been instructed as well because they rolled right into shimmying to "Rasputin" and one intrepid woman even tried a low Russian-style kicking dance move.

"Impressive," I called, bouncing my way slowly to the drinks table. I tucked my nice liquor away, not wanting to waste it on the sprite who would likely just dump it down his throat and burp in my face. Instead, I pulled out a punch bowl, dumped ice from a cooler into it, and poured a bottle of Meyers Dark Rum into the bowl. Next up, I opened a few bottles of lemonade and added it to the bowl.

"Rum and lemonade?" I called out and the women

danced over. I could see the sprite wanted some, but he kept zipping around the garden.

"I think he's suspicious after what happened in the wedding shop," Luna murmured at my ear when she came to collect her cup.

"Just gotta lull him into complacency. As of yet, we haven't been much of a threat to him, have we?"

"Nope."

"Hey, hey, hey…" I turned, singing along to the song. Dancing across the yard, I put a cup on a low table in the corner of my garden that held a garden light and a gnome statue on it. The sprite eyed me up, and I gave a nod to the table before dancing back to the group.

The dance party continued as the sun began to move toward the horizon. Since nothing seemed to be happening anytime soon, I started shaking my booty back toward the yet untouched pizza boxes. Maybe I would have time to just get a…

"Got him!" Luna crowed and I turned in shock.

The music immediately stopped and the women all rushed to crowd around where Luna and Abigail held their hands out in front of them, seeming to hold a magickal cord of connection to where the sprite lay unmoving on the ground, blinking up at them.

"Got you, you little…" Edna made a move to kick him but Miss Elva stopped her.

"Not a fair fight, honey. I know he done you bad with your shop and all, but we're better than that."

"Weren't you the one that slapped me in the face the other night?" Edna glared at her.

"Yeah, but you had control of all your faculties. You could've slapped me back, if you'd wanted to."

Edna surveyed Miss Elva's considerable girth and sniffed, deciding against commenting.

"What do we do now?" One of the women asked.

"We need to take him to the water," Luna said.

"And drown him." The same woman nodded sagely, and the sprite's eyes went wide.

"No, we aren't going to kill him. We just need to send him home," Luna said, a gentle smile on her lips. The sprite closed his eyes in obvious relief.

"Do we just pick him up?" Edna asked. I could see the bloodlust still in her eyes and I moved forward.

"I'll take him to the water. Is that the right thing to do, Luna?" I asked and she nodded. Bending over, I picked the little sprite up and cradled him like a baby, walking next to Luna and my mother to the water, with Miss Elva bringing up the rear. The sprite blinked up at me, worry in his eyes.

"Listen, buddy. You've caused a lot of problems here. This isn't the world for you. But I don't want to hurt you, okay? We're just going to send you home." Understanding seemed to slip through the sprite's eyes.

"Well, now what?" Edna asked as we all stood in a half-circle at my beach. The sun was just slipping under the horizon and the warm pink rays shot across the turquoise blue surface of the water. It was a calm night, with very little air movement, and the water lapped gently on the sand.

As one, the OGs turned to look at me and waited.

"What?" I said, looking at the women and then behind me. "Wait, you want *me* to do something?"

"This falls under your domain," Luna said softly.

"Um, I'm pretty sure it doesn't. Like…I've never even met a sprite before." The sprite and I looked at each other with equal trepidation. "Miss Elva backpacked with one. I'm sure she has a better idea of what to do here."

"Althea." Luna stepped forward and put a hand on my arm. "He needs the water to transport him to his realm. You, of all of us, will have better command of the ocean. You're a Sea Witch, remember? This is for you to do."

"What if I screw it up?" I mean, in all honesty, my track record was not good. I had a longer history of screwing up spells than I did with spells that resulted in positive outcomes.

"You won't." Luna promised me.

"You can do this, baby." My mom nodded to me over Luna's shoulder.

"You could do this with your eyes closed, child," Miss Elva said.

"Can you give me an idea of how to do a transport spell? You've got the book," I looked at Luna in desperation.

"Remember – intent in magick matters. But this is your magick. Your spell. You can design it how you want. It's just that you need to be clear what your intentions are."

"And my intentions are what again?" Sweat began to trickle down the back of my neck as I stared wide eyed at Luna.

"To send him to his realm. In one piece." Luna smiled again.

"But how do I know where his home is? What if I send him to Antarctica?"

"The magick will know," Luna promised.

"How are you so sure?"

"Because we've been practicing magick a long time," Miss Elva laughed. "Just use your powers. It'll be fine, I promise. If it's not, we'll fix it. I've grown attached to this little guy – he's got a nice sashay. We won't let any harm come to him, okay?"

I noticed the Star Society ladies kept quiet, likely because they didn't have enough experience to actually offer me advice. Taking a deep breath and letting it out slowly, I looked down at the sprite.

"Okay, you're a holy terror. But I don't wish you harm. So, if you have any magick that will also help you get home, now is the time to do it." The sprite blinked at me a few times as though to say he agreed, and I stepped forward.

"I mean, I can't just punt him into the water." I turned to Luna again. "He'll sink with the containment spell around him."

"Then think about how you would handle that." Luna advised.

Wow, talk about taking the training wheels off, I thought, mildly annoyed. Taking another deep breath I walked forward until I was standing in the water and the group of women faded behind me. It was just me, the ocean, and the sprite in my arms.

Thinking back to the other day where I had stood in this same spot and played with the water – making little water tornadoes and moving the water about – I focused on that image. Calling to the elements, with an extra push to the water, I felt what I now understood to be my magick ripple through me. Staring at the water, I mentally pushed it back until a small circle formed. I could see straight down to the sand below, while the water circled in column about two feet high. Once more, I met the sprite's eyes.

"I'll take care of you." I don't know where the certainty came from, but I knew in that moment, looking into his silvery eyes, that I could do this. I bent and placed him gently so he was standing upright in the column of water. Taking a few deep breaths, I called to the ocean, feeling its power flow into me and match the pulse of my heart beat for beat. As we merged together, the column of water began to spin faster around the sprite and I raised my hands to him.

It is my command
As mistress of the sea
Through water and land
The journey may be
To his vast magickal realm
Set this sprite free
And on the journey so
Safe home will you go.

I smiled at the sprite as my power surrounded him, and he winked out of sight before the water converged onto the sand.

"Safe home will you go," I whispered once more, touching my hand to my heart. The power of the ocean pulsed through me and I felt a funny little zing and then peacefulness flooded me. The sprite had made it to his realm.

"He's made it."

I turned to the group on the beach and they exploded in

cheers. Blinking, I realized that I was deeply moved by what had just happened.

"You did it!" Miss Elva cheered, and the women pulled me into a hug, dancing in a circle around me, and I blinked at the tears that flooded my eyes.

I'd done it. I'd stepped into my power and I'd handled the problem instead of creating a bigger one. Hesitantly, I glanced over my shoulder at the ocean just to make sure I hadn't created a massive sprite sea monster or something. When the waters remained calm, I sighed in relief.

"Okay, who wants pizza?"

Chapter Twenty-Two

PIZZA WAS the cure for everything, in my opinion.

Instead of dissolving into a sobbing mess because I'd finally figured out my powers and had actually owned them, I'd devoured a piece of pizza—okay three pieces—and was happily swaying to the music after I'd finished a glass of rum and lemonade. The rest of the ladies had left after pizza except for Edna, who now walked over to where we sat on the back porch with her bag in hand.

"I wanted to offer my apologies. You ladies have all given me a lot to think about, and I promise I won't take any of these lessons lightly."

"What she needs to think about are those stuffed dead cats in her hallway," Rosita hissed in my ear, and I bit back a laugh. Rosita had appeared after the sprite had been delivered home – wisely staying away from my yard when I was practicing magick. My heart twisted at the thought of Rafe. I hoped I'd be able to bring him back for Miss Elva. No, I *would* bring him back.

"As I said...we all make mistakes." Miss Elva shrugged and sipped her Corona.

"I just hope that this can release you from some hurts of the past and that you can move forward to a healthier and happier future." Mom smiled at Edna and toasted her with her drink.

"I think I'll be able to. I already feel lighter," Edna admitted. "But I do have one last thing I need to clear up before I can move forward."

"What's that?" Miss Elva asked. I had a feeling I knew what it would be and kept my eyes on Miss Elva's face. When Edna pulled the necklace from her bag, Miss Elva's face flooded with pure joy.

"My necklace!"

"Yes. And as a token of my appreciation for your help with my, um, personal growth, I've anonymously paid the outstanding bill for you."

Of course she had to pay it anonymously, I thought. There was still a matter of the whole armed robbery she could be charged with.

"It's a little damaged. From the spell. But that's just the gold. The stone is perfectly in shape. It's a four-carat star sapphire and one of the best I've seen."

Miss Elva took the necklace and her face filled with wonder.

"This was my mother's."

"What?" I cried. We all looked to Miss Elva in shock. She rarely spoke of her family.

"Did you know that?" Luna asked.

"No, I can feel it now though. It explains why I was so

obsessed with getting this necklace. I mean, I love my sparkles and all, but this one really called to me."

"If I had known…" Edna shook her head and shrugged. "Actually, I can't say what I would have done. I'm just glad I can deliver it back to you."

"Thank you. I mean it." Miss Elva blinked rapidly, and I realized she was fighting tears. Now I'd seen everything, I thought. She cleared her throat rapidly and when Edna turned to leave, Miss Elva stopped her. "Edna?"

"Yes?" Edna turned.

"Maybe we could get together sometime? I have a huge fashion line I'm about to launch. But we don't have a bridal line yet. Maybe you'd be interested in collaborating?"

Well, you could about knock me over with a feather, I thought, as I stared wide-eyed at the two former enemies. It just went to show you – change was always possible.

A smile bloomed on Edna's face. "I'd like that."

Edna left just as Trace, my father, and Hank were entering the front door. I'd texted Trace as soon as I'd gotten my pizza and had patted myself on the back for being a good girlfriend. Now, seeing him stride across my living area, a smile on his face and Hank on his heels, I was more certain than ever that he was my future.

"All good?" Trace asked, brushing a quick kiss on my lips and wrapping an arm around me.

"All good," I said.

My dad immediately plopped down next to my mom and they curled into each other and murmured softly.

"There's pizza." I pointed to the table where the boxes of pizza were, and Trace beelined for it, Hank on his heels.

"I love that beast," Rosita sighed and I narrowed my eyes at her.

"The dog," she laughed.

I dropped down next to Luna, and she squeezed my arm.

"Good job today. I'm proud of you," Luna said.

"Thanks. It feels good." I turned to her. "Listen, I feel like I've made a lot of big decisions quickly, so I'm going to keep rolling with it. I'm taking my mother's advice."

Mom perked up and leaned forward, and Miss Elva stopped gazing at her necklace to turn to me.

"I'm going to cut my days to two days a week doing readings. I'll raise my prices and only give readings to people who genuinely appreciate them. Sometimes I still feel like I'm a bit of a circus oddity. People book appointments just to laugh at me or test my strength. Mom's right. The higher my prices, the more seriously people will take me. Plus, I've saved a lot. I can afford to drop my hours. Then with my free time, I'll help you in the store and work on my photography."

"Which means more dives with me." Trace's grin was wide in his face.

"Yes, though I'll pay you," I said to Trace and he laughed, shaking his head at me like I was crazy.

"Like I'd let you."

"Well, we can figure something out. But if Beau is serious about this gallery of his, well, then I need to get more serious about my work."

"What gallery?" Dad asked and I filled him in on Beau's idea. He'd been in a conversation the other night at Lucky's and must have missed that news.

"I swear whatever that kid invests in is wildly successful. You'll do great there," Dad assured me.

"This feels good. It feels right. Like I can balance my life better."

"It sounds like everyone has had some big changes this week," Luna looked around. "Trace and Althea back together. Abigail and I working on a tonic line together. Miss Elva working with Edna."

"And what about you?" Miss Elva looked at Luna. "Do you have any changes you'd like to add to your life? It's a potent full moon tomorrow – a good time for manifesting."

"I mean…my life is full. I'm happy. Mathias is amazing…" Luna's tone trailed off wistfully. "Though I do wish he could spend more time with us. But that's the nature of being with a doctor. I heard they are hiring more doctors, though, so I think I'll actually get a chance to have him around more."

"I hope you told Edna to hold that dress for you," Miss Elva observed. "It looked like liquid moonlight. It could have been made for you."

"I made a note," Luna laughed.

"In all seriousness though," Miss Elva sobered. She crossed her arms over her chest and eyed me. "The full moon's tomorrow."

"Rafe," I said, meeting her eyes.

"I miss him, Althea. I know he drove you crazy. And I know he can be rude at times. But he's my rude pirate. Will you bring him back for me?"

"I will do my best," I promised. "So long as you both can lead me in the spell. I feel much more confident in my power now."

"Then we'll meet tomorrow. At Lucky's and do it there."

"Why at Lucky's?" I glanced toward my beach. "Shouldn't we do it here? We lost him here."

"Because I want the fried pickles. And, Rafe loves Lucky's. He's a worse gossip than I am. He loves to sneak up on everyone."

"Alright, I'll call Beau and see if we can do it after he shuts the restaurant down. He closes at ten on Thursdays anyway."

"Plan for it."

Pleading exhaustion, Luna and Miss Elva left and my parents disappeared to the guest room. That left Trace and I to cozy up on the couch while Hank dropped the tennis ball repeatedly in Trace's lap. When my phone rang, I almost ignored it.

"It's Mathias," Trace said. He handed me the phone. I couldn't ignore his call.

"Hey! Is everything okay?" It wasn't often that Mathias called me.

"Hi, yes." I could hear the sounds of the hospital in the background and then a door closing and silence. "Listen… I'm sorry, I don't have a ton of time, but I wanted to ask you a question. Luna said you're doing a ritual or something tomorrow night on the full moon."

"We are, yes. At Lucky's."

"Well, I hadn't really planned for that. I mean, I could push this off to another time. But, I had someone study an astrology chart for me. And it was supposed to be this moon. And that was my plan. But my shift isn't over until ten. And…"

"Mathias. Stop. You're absolutely making no sense. What had you planned to do?" I laughed.

"I was going to propose tomorrow. But...I don't want to interrupt this ritual. It sounds pretty important to Miss Elva. I guess I can wait?" His voice sounded pained. My heart did a little dance in my chest and I bit back a squeal.

"No! You have to! Listen – we'll do the ritual. It won't take long. Miss Elva will be happy as can be. And Lucky's has that lovely outdoor area where you can go beneath the palm trees with the moon and the water in the background. If you want, I can talk to Beau and we'll go get candles lit and make it all pretty for you. It'll be perfect. Of course, you should propose under the full moon."

"You're sure?" Mathias asked.

"I'm totally sure. It'll be amazing. I'm so happy!" I exclaimed. With promises to touch base tomorrow, Mathias clicked off.

"So, he's taking the plunge, huh?" Trace slung his arm over my shoulder and pulled me into his side.

"Yes! I'm so happy. They are perfect for each other." I sighed in happiness, letting my head fall against Trace's chest.

"Do you want to do that?" Trace asked, pressing his lips to my head.

"What? Get married?"

"Yes, do you want to get married? To me?"

"Are you proposing to me, Trace?" I teased lightly, though my heart shivered at his words.

"Unofficially, *yes*, I am. I'll do a fancy one later. But it just works, Althea. I want you in my life forever. You're my best friend and you're the first person I want to tell things to. I missed you when you were gone. I miss you every day when I'm not with you, actually. I loved that you kept checking in with me today. I love you, Althea. I loved you as a friend first, and then as a lover, and now I want you as a life partner."

I blew out a shaky breath as I turned and met his eyes. I hadn't thought I wanted marriage, and yet now I could see how simple it could be.

"Unofficially, right? Because we can't take away from Luna's excitement."

"Unofficially, but officially. I promise I'll give you a proper proposal down the road. This will just be our little secret." A sexy smile quirked Trace's lips and I lost myself in his ocean-blue eyes for a moment.

"Yes, Trace, I want a life with you. As messy and weird and amazing as it will be. It won't be normal, but it will always be fascinating and frustrating…and just right."

Trace kissed me gently, and I sank into the kiss, everything falling neatly into place in my life.

A soggy tennis ball landed splat in my lap, and I pulled back, laughing down at a grinning Hank.

"Actually, this might just be the perfect proposal for me after all."

Chapter Twenty-Three

TRACE and I trooped into Lucky's an hour before close. I'd spent the day seeing my clients and writing up a notice to send out to my client list about my adjusted prices as well as my new office hours. For the next few months, I would have to honor current client appointments, but then I'd be able to fully switch over to my new schedule.

After Trace's secret proposal the night before, we'd stayed the night at his house, snuggled up in bed and enjoying each other's touch. It seemed silly to leave my house, but at the same time – I just couldn't bring myself to be intimate with Trace while my parents were under the same roof. Which might pose a problem since they planned to stay longer. For now, we'd agreed more nights at Trace's house, and we'd see how things went. I suspected, at some point, that my parents would want their own space as well and they'd rent a condo for a while.

For now, I was all but floating with joy.

"Well, now. I can't tell you how delighted I am to see you both. Together." Beau beamed at us over the bar he was wiping down with a towel. Tonight, he had a misty blue t-shirt on that set off his eyes nicely.

"I am, too," I smiled at him. We'd been talking back and forth all day about Luna's proposal and had made a little plan for it.

"Good. Don't screw this one up, Althea. You're too old for this drama."

"Excuse me?" I raised an eyebrow at him. "You're dating a new guy like every other week."

"Yeah, but that's just fun. And good sex. My heart's not in it.. But you two, well…you were starting to hurt each other. A lot. So, knock it off, okay?"

"I promise. It's knocked off. We're good."

"That's what I like to hear. Now, I've got Ava on drinks. I'm going to steal your woman for a rendezvous on the beach now," Beau said, grabbing my arm and pulling me across the bar. Since it was close to closing time, only half the tables were full, and I nodded at a few familiar faces.

"I found the perfect spot. She won't see it until he backs her up into it. The only thing will be the candles. As soon as she sees the candlelight, she'll know. But I was thinking maybe I could wait until I know she said yes and then flick fairy lights on instead?" Beau drew me to a small cluster of palm trees that formed a semi-circle and faced the water. The moon had just risen over the water and it cast its light across the beach. Beau had scattered flowers everywhere, creating almost an illusion as though we were standing on a cloud. "See the lights strung between the trees?"

"I can just make out the strands. Oh, Beau," I clenched

his arm. "This is incredible. I feel like I'm on a cloud of flowers. I think forget the candles, yeah? The moonlight is so lovely against the petals. And then, yes, maybe flick the fairy lights on after she accepts?"

"Perfect. Then I think we're done here. I love this stuff!" Beau gushed and dragged me back inside. He was already talking about what he'd wear to the wedding, and I laughed, hushing him when I saw Luna at the bar.

"Hi! Where were you two?" Luna asked. She looked perfect, as usual, in a simple white sundress with a turquoise beaded necklace around her throat and silver bangles at her wrist.

"Just checking out the ritual space," I said quickly. "Moon's coming up and looks great. Once the restaurant clears out, we'll be good."

"Should I go check..." Luna asked and then smiled when Beau stopped in front of her.

"White wine?"

"After the ritual, please. Alcohol and magick don't mix well," Luna said.

"There's the rest of them. I'll get some fried pickles out asap." Beau shot a worried look at Miss Elva who was already scanning the bar for food.

"Hello, you look nice," I said to Miss Elva. She also wore white tonight. Her caftan was shot through with silver threads, giving an iridescent look to the material, and she'd hung sparkly feathered earrings at her ears.

"I wanted to look good for my honey. I've been missing him."

"He'll be back soon enough. I even studied the spells that Luna gave me to read up on." I patted my purse where

I'd tucked the spells away. My parents greeted Beau with kisses and so did Miss Elva when she saw the large baskets of fried pickles.

By the time our meals had come, the place had emptied out and the last of the servers were wiping up the table. Beau had sent the kitchen staff home early and it was just us when someone knocked at the glass door.

"Oh, that's Mathias. He'd said he'd meet us here." Luna hopped up and went to get him. They returned, holding hands, and a faint pink tinged Luna's cheeks. He must have kissed her senseless, I mused, a little smile on my face.

"Hello everyone," Mathias said. Tall, broad shouldered, and absolutely dreamy, Mathias could be any woman's dream man. But I knew his heart was pure gold, which is why I loved him for Luna. It didn't matter how many women simpered over him; he'd never have eyes for another. I introduced Mathias to my parents and then Miss Elva cleared her throat.

"Right, let's get on with it. Miss Elva is missing her honey," I declared. Nerves skittered through me as we all trooped outside, but I worked on my breathing and reminded myself that just yesterday I had commanded an ocean to deliver a sprite to another realm. I most certainly could bring a pirate ghost back to Miss Elva. Plus, I didn't even have to do the ritual on my own. We'd all been a part of the spell that I'd screwed up. I just needed to be a part of it and use my magick to pull him back.

Feeling confident for the first time ever, I steered Luna away from where we'd set up her proposal spot.

"Oh, but wouldn't it be better down there? Closer to

the beach?" Luna worried her lip as she studied the dark area I'd pulled her to. "The light is better over there."

"On it," Beau called, and in moments he'd brought over two tiki torches and planted them in the ground before disappearing back into the restaurant.

"I guess that works…" Luna looked around.

"I'm happy with this. Enough stalling. The lovely moon is up and calling to us. We'll be at our most powerful and can bring Rafe home. Shall we?" Flames danced off the reflection of Miss Elva's eyes and I nodded quickly.

Luna dropped to the ground and drew a circle, which we all promptly stepped into. I wasn't sure why I didn't have to draw a circle for my magick, but I was starting to really understand what they meant about magick not boxing you in. When it came down to it, we were all magick. We just had to figure out what our own particular brand was. It was the little things, too, I realized. People were always talking about big magick and big power – but there was so much power in the little magicks as well, I realized. Little magicks like always being able to make a perfect recipe. Or the ability to bring a smile to someone's face. Or in my case – to take a photo and share the beautiful ocean with someone who'd never seen it before. Maybe life wasn't full of big magick, but instead was a tapestry of little magicks all woven together.

"Althea?" Luna whispered and I snapped back to reality, stepping neatly into the circle and clasping hands with Miss Elva and Luna as they called the elements. This time, I could feel the power surround us when the circle was protected, and I understood now how this was such a tangible practice for Luna and Miss Elva. Focusing on the intent to bring Rafe home, I looked out to the ocean and opened myself to the flow of the power. As it zipped through me, both women squeezed my hands tighter, acknowledging the extra magick that I was adding to the spell, and happiness flooded me. I was helping – I was making a difference. And that was something that really mattered.

We cross the veil
To look for a soul
We'd like to hail
We'd like him whole
For he is missed
Deliver Dear Rafe to us
So he may be kissed.

I mean, as spells went, I supposed it would do – and it wasn't like I was some great poet anyway. Focusing on Rafe's image, I kept my power flowing and closed my eyes, hoping against hope that he hadn't gone too far through the veil and into the next realm.

"Come on, Rafe. Get your butt back here. Miss Elva misses you," I muttered.

"But you don't?" Rafe whispered sweetly at my ear and I jumped.

"Don't break the circle," Luna ordered, holding tight to my hand and I waited while she finished the spell and released us from the magick. Once free, I stepped back and turned to give Rafe my usual attitude.

He shocked me by floating over and brushing a kiss against my cheek. It felt like the flutter of butterfly wings, but I still felt it.

"Thank you for bringing me home, Althea. I realize I've been harsh with you and I shouldn't have been. I promise to work on that in the future."

"Rafe! Life in the veil has changed you," I said, tilting my head at the pirate ghost in surprise.

"I missed you guys. But more than anything, I missed my lovemountain." Rafe swooped to Miss Elva and fluttered around her while they whispered…well…I walked away quickly before I could hear anything they were whispering.

"Honestly, I'm glad that went so well. I was convinced I might screw it up too and then, well, Miss Elva would hate me forever."

"You've claimed your magick, Althea. Once you step into that, everything changes, don't you see?" Luna smiled up at me. "Could you feel a difference in that spell?"

"I could. I really could. Not only could I feel my own power, but I felt a wall of it around us when you put the circle up. I get why some of this stuff comes so easily to you now. It's like…a tangible thing. I felt like I could reach out and touch it."

"And once you have that understanding of your magick, you'll be able to be much better at spell work. Things will come more intuitively to you as well." Luna looked up as Mathias strolled to her and put an arm around her shoulder. "I guess we should probably go. Mathias has had a pretty long day."

"I have. But it's such a pretty night…I was wondering if you'd like to stroll along the water before we go? I know how much you love the full moon."

"I really do," Luna laughed, "I mean…it's in my name and all."

"Go ahead you guys, I'm going to tell my parents that the ritual went well." I couldn't even bring myself to look at Mathias and took off for the restaurant. Once inside, I skidded to a stop by the bar.

"How'd it go, kiddo?" Dad asked.

"Perfect. Great. Oh it's happening! They are walking down to the beach now!" I whispered excitedly.

"Should we go spy on them? Maybe take a picture so they have it?" I asked, turning to Beau.

"No," Mom said emphatically. "Luna will feel you near. Let them have this private moment to themselves. You can take a picture after."

"You're right. But how will we know when it's over?" Beau demanded. "I wanted to put the fairy lights on."

"Just chill. Here, have a drink." Dad handed Beau his beer bottle and he drank it down without thinking.

I took a big gulp of the Moscow mule that Beau had made for me and leaned into Trace as we waited. All of a sudden, I felt this warm wave of happiness rush over me and I knew…I just knew…that Luna was engaged. Mom met my eyes and nodded.

"Fairy lights, Beau."

"Oh, now! Oh, shit!" Beau ran to the back room and flipped the lights on and we all raced outside to see. I'd brought my nice camera for this and Miss Elva and the two ghosts joined us as we walked down to where the palm trees were lit up with an intricate web of fairy lights and the flower petals coated the ground like a waxen cloud. Luna and Mathias stood in the middle of the cloud, swaying gently together as he kissed her, the moon full in the background. I fired off a dozen shots before they turned and saw us – Luna holding up her hand.

"We're engaged!"

"Congrats!" Everyone cried. I hung back, wanting to capture the moment, and took picture after picture until Luna squealed and pulled me into a hug.

"Let me see the ring," I demanded, blinking back tears.

"It's a moonstone," Luna said, holding out her hand. A moonstone, set in rose gold and circled in not one, but two layers of chunky diamonds, shimmered on her finger.

"It's perfect for you. Well done, sir." I smiled to Mathias and wiped a tear from my cheek with the back of my hand.

"Now we're both engaged," Luna whispered happily in my ear and I drew back, my mouth hanging open.

"But...how did you know?" I hissed, grabbing her arm and keeping my voice low. "It's not even official. This is your day, Luna. Don't even bring it up."

"I bet you felt a wave of love when Mathias proposed to me, right?" I nodded at her, not comprehending.

"Did you think I wouldn't feel the same when Trace proposed to you? We're linked, you know. Sisters."

"The OG Gang," Miss Elva stepped up, and nodded.

"Wait," I stepped back and looked at everyone smiling at me. "You all know?"

"Of course we do, honey. We were just letting you take your time to tell us."

"But this is their day. Not mine. I don't want to take away from..." Miss Elva gripped my shoulders and turned me around and I found Trace on one knee in the blanket of flowers, a ring box in his hand.

"Oh my…you got a ring? When?"

"Show a little appreciation, geez. In my days, women would kill for a ring," Rafe complained at my ear.

"So lovely to have you back, Rafe," I said and stepped forward to where Trace smiled up at me.

"You didn't have to do this," I said. "I was happy with last night."

"I did have to do this. And I wanted to do this. And how much more official can it be than with your parents watching? Althea Rose, will you do me the world's greatest honor and become my wife?"

"Hardly an honor," Rafe said and then Miss Elva quickly shut him up before I could send him back through the veil.

"I absolutely would be delighted to."

Trace offered me the ring box and I opened it, tears pouring from my eyes as I saw the sapphire ring nestled on the silk.

"Sapphire for the ocean that brought us together," I said, understanding instantly what he'd meant by choosing that stone.

"Exactly. Can I get off my knee now?" Trace asked and I pulled him up, kissing him deeply before turning to smile at everyone.

"A double engagement!" Beau fanned his face. "Does this mean a double wedding because you all are going to send me into hyperventilation."

"We can talk about that. For now…drinks!" Miss Elva declared, and we all swept inside to belly up to the bar. We talked for hours, shooting down Rafe's idea of a pirate-themed wedding, and considering Rosita's idea of a beach-themed wedding. Beau and I talked more deeply about the gallery and I told him how I planned to change my hours and devote myself more seriously to my photography. I couldn't remember when I'd had so much fun.

Leaning into Trace's side, I smiled up at my fiancé.

"Do you want one more?" Beau asked from the other side of the bar.

"No," I said, relaxing into Trace's side, while my friends and family laughed and chattered around me. "I'm good."

Epilogue

One Year Later

"OW!" I said as Miss Elva poked a pin into my hair. I glared at her from where I sat in my bedroom, wishing that I'd decided to elope. If I'd had any idea the hysteria that surrounded the planning of a wedding, I would never have agreed to marry Trace. We would have been equally as happy living as life partners without all of this extra fuss.

"Hush. It's gonna be a fine party, and you'll be happy you did it this way," Miss Elva promised as she stepped back and studied her work. "I really like what you've done with your hair color."

"You don't think it's too much?" I brought my hand to my curls. Last week I'd taken the plunge and dyed them with a mermaid theme in mind – and the colors varying pinks blending into deep purple with a touch of turquoise highlights mixed in. It looked like the sun dancing off a mermaid's tail, and I couldn't be happier with it.

"It's perfect. Plus, against that pretty lace dress of Edna's, it will look stunning, but also unique and funky. Which is who you are. There." Miss Elva stepped back and put her hands on her hips, studying me. "Just right."

"Can I see?"

"Of course, child." Miss Elva stepped back and I went to stand in front of the mirror. I was worried when I asked if she would help with hair and makeup that I'd end up with a bedazzled turban and feather earrings, but I had to hand it to her – Miss Elva knew her stuff. My hair was arranged in artful tumbling curls and she'd tucked small pins with tiny clusters of rhinestones throughout my hair to pin back various curls. The effect made my hair shimmer and dance under the light, but it wasn't over the top. For my makeup, she'd done a lovely shadowy eye and then had glued one little crystal at the corner of each eye for a pop.

"Have I told you how amazing you are?"

"Yes, but keep telling me," Miss Elva moved to where my dress hung. "Are you ready for this?"

"Is Luna ready? I don't want to put my dress on if she isn't."

True to our double engagement, we'd decided to do a double wedding with only our nearest and dearest in attendance. The ceremony was taking place under the full moon in my backyard by the beach. Afterwards, Beau had closed Lucky's for the night and we would have a massive reception and dance the night away.

"Luna," Miss Elva called, poking her head out of my door. "How close are you to putting your dress on?"

"Almost done. I'll bring it in and we can dress together," Luna's sweet voice echoed back.

"Okay, let's get Mr. Handsome ready and then I'll put my dress on." Miss Elva and my mother were serving as bridesmaids and you would have thought the two of them had been tasked with planning a royal wedding. The amount of times I had to look at material swatches for their dresses before I had banned them from ever showing me a sample again had been in the hundreds, but it had felt like thousands. I didn't even know what they'd settled on, but Miss Elva had her fashion line produce it. That move had led to opening a bridesmaid's division and she'd had to hire a bigger team.

Elva, the fashion line, had finally come to fruition and exploded onto the fashion scene just as Miss Elva had expected it would. Celebrities all over the world were draping themselves in her sparkling caftans and taking photos of themselves in exotic locations. It was a surprise Miss Elva had even had time to participate in this wedding with how busy she was. That being said, Miss Elva had turned out to be a brilliant CEO. She ran a tight ship, delegated masterfully, and her next collection was highly anticipated. Rafe, true to his nature, was still a pain in my butt, but he'd softened with me a bit this past year. Perhaps it had been the scare of disappearing forever into the veil, or perhaps we'd just reached an uneasy truce. But either way, I found him significantly more tolerable now.

"Oh, ladies in their underwear. My favorite," Rafe floated into my bedroom.

"Out, Rafe." Did I say I liked him more?

"I was just checking to see if my lovemountain needed anything?" Rafe glared at me.

"How is everything downstairs, Rafe?" Miss Elva asked.

"Everything looks to be exactly as you want it, my lovemountain."

"I notice he said how *you* wanted it – not us brides." I laughed.

"Well, really, at some point it was just best that you surrendered everything to us." Miss Elva shrugged. "Rafe, go on downstairs and tell Abigail to stop fussing with the flowers. We're almost ready."

"Oh, Althea, you look lovely," Luna stopped at the door.

"Luna! Oh my goddess!" Luna had pulled the top half of her hair back with a simple moonstone band and the rest of her hair fell in a smooth column behind her. Her makeup was minimal, but she was so gorgeous she really needed none anyway. Holding her dress in hand, she hung it on the hook next to mine and came over to grab my hands.

"I'm so happy for us. How do you feel?"

"I feel good. All of this feels good. Even if I'm not one for a big ceremony," I admitted.

"Sometimes the ceremony makes it special. And we're doing it our way."

"We are. I like that."

"Ladies – it's dress time."

"Do we finally get to see your dresses?" I wouldn't be surprised if my mother and Miss Elva outshone us both.

"I believe so. There you go, Mr. Handsome." Miss Elva finished putting Hank into a little vest and red tartan bowtie. "Aren't you just the most handsome ever?" Hank immediately rolled over on his back and put his paws in the air, inviting a belly scratch. "Most men roll over for me darling."

"Oh, are we ready?" Abigail poked her head into the room, a dress bag in her hand.

"We are ready. But I swear to goddess if you pull an Ovary Gang dress out of that bag, then you are both out of the wedding." I glared at Miss Elva and she held her hand to her chest like she was shocked.

"I would never."

"Mmhmm. Okay, let's do this."

"Brides first," Mom declared and soon I was being turned and manhandled like a piece of meat getting prepared for the grill. "Arm's up!"

Dutifully I put my arms up and they slid the dress over my head and down my body. Zipping it up, I turned to look at Luna and blinked at the tears that sprang to my eyes.

"You will not cry and mess up my hard work with your makeup," Miss Elva ordered.

"Okay, okay, okay." I waved my hands in front of my eyes. "Luna, you look like an angel."

"And you look like a sexy Sea Witch," Luna beamed back at me.

"You both are stunning. I couldn't be prouder." My mom wrapped an arm around me, careful not to mess up my makeup, and hugged me. I could feel the warmth of her love radiate through me and I took a few deep breaths to steady myself. "Are you okay, honey? Do you need one of my stomach tonics?"

"No, I'm just fine," I said. Abigail and Luna's tonics for anxiety and other issues had exploded and their website was now by waiting-list-only. I knew after the wedding they planned to expand their team. My parents had stayed with me for a month, but as I had suspected, they decided to rent their own space. My father had flown to Ireland and bought the cottage of his dreams, and my mother had rented a condo in Tequila Key. They'd split the time between the two places over the past year and I don't think I'd ever seen them happier. As was I. I'd spent the year getting the gallery up and running with Beau, seeing to clients, helping Luna with her line, and spending stolen moments under water with Trace. I had zero complaints about my life.

"Our turn! I can't wait for you to see these!" Abigail laughed. "Close your eyes."

Dutifully we did and there was a lot of fussing and muttering before we were finally allowed to see their masterpieces.

"You've outdone yourself," I whispered to Miss Elva. The dresses were midnight blue, made with soft sheer tulle and netting. Cut in a simple scoop neck style and an A-line skirt, they'd lined the second layer of the skirt with sequined midnight netting, so when they twirled the skirts shimmered in the light.

"I didn't want to go too sparkly, seeing as it's not my day," Miss Elva said. "So, we went with subdued sparkle. Though you know I had to add my necklace." The star sapphire necklace shone beautifully around Miss Elva's neck. I was fairly certain she hadn't taken it off since the jeweler had repaired it for her.

"You both look fantastic." I meant it, too. "In fact, we all do."

"I have one more gift for us to wear." Miss Elva bent and picked up a bag and handed us each a silver-wrapped box.

"What are these?" Luna asked.

"You don't have to wear them if it doesn't suit your style today, but I thought you might like them. Go on, open them up," Miss Elva ushered.

"Oh…I love it." I laughed out loud – I couldn't help it. They were an intricately twisted gold chain bracelet with delicate diamond initials strung in the middle. The initials were: OG.

"I'm wearing mine." I couldn't stop laughing. We all clasped our bracelets together and brought our hands together in the middle. The jewelry was classy, subtle, and added just a touch of sparkle at our wrists.

"Ovary Gang!" Miss Elva crowed. "Take 'em down!"

And so, we went downstairs to find our men and do just that.

*Be sure to read the author's note for some free tequila!

Author's Note

Well, my friends, our journey with Althea and the gang has finally come to an end. It is a little bittersweet to say farewell to this world that I've created, but I felt like this is where their story needed to end. If a new story knocks on the door to my mind one day...perhaps we'll revisit Tequila Key. Or, you never know, maybe one day we'll follow Miss Elva on her adventures.

Writing Althea's story has been a joyful one for me. At times, she's frustrated me with her inability to learn or grow – and sometimes I've wondered if that was a mirror image of when I felt stuck at certain points in my life. Althea's grown with me through the years, and I like to think she's learned a few major life lessons – as I have – along the way.

So, I will leave you with this, my friends – don't forget to fill your life with little magicks. We're so very lucky to be here and if you try hard enough, I guarantee you can find something magickal each and every day.

Sparkle on... Tricia xoxo

Author update: Free Tequila!

Well...as you know me by now, I couldn't resist revisiting Tequila Key for a delightful Christmas romp with Miss Elva. Download this free Christmas story and enjoy Miss

Elva finally debuting her fashion line all while trying to solve a late-night mystery.

head on over to my website to download.
https://www.triciaomalley.com/free

I hope my books have added a little magick into your life. If you have a moment to add some to my day, you can help by telling your friends and leaving a review. Word-of-mouth is the most powerful way to share my stories. Thank you.

One Way Ticket

A PERFECT ROMANTIC SUMMER BEACH READ

New from Tricia O'Malley
Read Today

NY Times & USA Today bestselling author, Tricia O'Malley's latest romance is a funny and heart-pounding story where booking a one-way ticket to paradise means starting over, letting go, and taking a chance on love...one more time.

Feel Good Read

"In today's world of loud voices and nasty divisions, it is wonderful to find something soothing and familiar to remind us of what really matters. This book brings us back to a time when we all could believe in innate goodness, kindness and love. It is a wonderful and refreshing reminder that we need."

GrumpyGranny - *5 out of 5 stars*

The following is a sneak peak of Chapter One.

Enjoy.

Chapter 1

THE DOOR WAS LOCKED.

Paige jiggled the handle, confused, because her boyfriend Horatio subscribed to an open-door policy. This welcoming attitude and willingness to trust others was what had originally drawn Paige to him. Sometimes she felt like his mother, trying to caution Horatio to protect his interests, but he'd just laugh, pat her on the head, and tell her she worried too much. If she pressed an issue, Horatio would pull her to bed and make her forget what had ever bothered her to begin with.

Maddening at times? Sure. But fun? It certainly was. It made the responsibilities that weighed heavily on her shoulders each day seem less of a burden and more a badge of honor. Especially when the other yoga students at the studio gazed her way, envy in their eyes, when Horatio wrapped his arms around Paige and insisted his students defer to her for all their scheduling needs. "In time, my goddess, in time," Horatio would say, soothing her worries away.

Finally finding her key, she unlocked the door and pushed it open, hanging her tote on a hook by the door. The front door opened directly into a small main living area, with a tiny but efficient kitchen done in white on white, tucked to the side. Two doors led from opposite sides of the main living area, each leading to generous sized bedrooms with attached baths. One of the rooms they'd converted into an office and Paige poked her head in there first. A sigh escaped her as she surveyed the mess of papers that had been dropped onto her desk while Horatio's remained immaculate except for his sleek little computer, a bowl of crystals, and a large framed photo of himself in warrior pose. Turning, Paige left the room and opened the door to their shared bedroom.

"Oh my god!" Paige gasped, her hand to her mouth, as she took in the tangle of limbs and...so much nakedness... on her bed. *Their* bed.

"Paige, my goddess, you're home," Horatio smiled to her from where he leaned against the cushioned headboard, one *she'd* picked out, and sliced a sliver of an apple with his ritual knife. He handed the slice of apple to one of the current teachers-in-training, Lily, who was curled at one side. On the other, Nadia, also an instructor in the same class, stretched languidly and smiled at Paige like she'd just inked the deal on a well-padded prenuptial agreement.

Everyone was naked.

"I *am* home. The...the door was locked..." Paige said, feeling stupid as they all stared at her like *she* was the intruder. Nobody made a move to get up or even exhibit any type of chagrin. If anything, Lily looked annoyed at Paige for interrupting.

"It was? That's odd," Horatio mused, stretching his tanned limbs out – a spray tan, at that – and offered a slice of apple to Nadia.

"I locked it, Horatio." Nadia batted her eyelashes up at Horatio while Paige tried to breathe through the murder fantasies currently playing out in her head.

"Now, Nadia, you know that's unacceptable. Having an open-door policy is very important to me," Horatio said, his voice stern, and turned to hand her piece of apple over to Lily instead. Pushing her lush lower lip out, Nadia picked at a wrinkle in the sheet.

"I thought it was for the best."

"I'll have to punish you, as you well know," Horatio sighed, and laid his hand across her bum, spanking Nadia enough to make a small squeak emanate from her perfect doll-like mouth but not enough to leave a mark.

"Excuse me," Paige said, drawing their attention back to her, "but what the hell is going on here?"

"What does it look like?" Lily giggled, winding a leg around Horatio's and smiling up at Paige. It hurt to see them so casually wrapped around Horatio, but Paige couldn't decide if it was because they were younger and bendier, or because Horatio was cheating on her, which probably said something about the current nature of her relationship.

Paige filed that thought away to examine more deeply on another day when she wasn't confronted with a smorgasbord of boobs and butts on her favorite sateen sheets.

"Both of you…out!" Paige ordered, pointing to the women, and it was a credit to her patience that she didn't grab for Horatio's ritual knife when they both looked to him for guidance instead of listening to Paige's command first.

"You look tense, my goddess. Why don't you join us?" Horatio asked.

"I'm sorry…what?" Paige stood there, mouth hanging open, feeling like she'd walked into a play that she didn't have the script for.

"Join us, please," Horatio said, his blue eyes crinkling at the corner as he smiled at her and patted the bed. "It will relax you."

"You can't be serious," Paige said, heart hammering in her chest, as her world tilted on its axis.

"Please, my goddess, join us. You'll feel wonderful after. I'm certain we can loosen that dark energy in your third chakra. I can feel it from here."

Paige's eyebrows almost hit her hairline.

"My chakras? You're concerned about my chakras right now?"

"Seriously, Paige, we've been meaning to talk to you about them anyway," Lily sniffed, and Paige zeroed in on her.

"I'm sorry…what?" Paige said, feeling like a parrot squawking the only phrase it knew.

"Your chakras. They've become a bit of a problem at the studio."

"It's bringing us all down," Nadia confirmed.

"I think I'm going to take a shower." Lily yawned and

reached for a pink robe next to the bed. Paige's pink robe. She'd saved for weeks for that robe and was pleased when she finally decided to splurge on herself.

"You and you," Paige said, finally jumping into action and grabbing each of the women's arms, "get out!" Pulling them unceremoniously from the bed, she bent and picked up discarded clothes, tossing them into the living room, and shoved the astounded girls from the bedroom before slamming the door in their faces.

"Hey! My iPhone's in there!" Nadia yelled.

Paige turned and locked the door.

"Not feeling like sharing? That's fine. You only had to say so, my goddess. No need to get rough with the girls." Horatio stretched before standing and turning toward the bathroom.

"Nope," Paige said, blocking his path and forcing him to step back until his butt hit the bed again. Looking up at her, he pinched his nose and sighed.

"Paige, I guess it's time I talk to you about this. It's something I should've brought up earlier…"

"*This* being the fact that you're cheating on me?" Paige crossed her arms over her chest and glared down at him. His golden hair was tucked into his usual man-bun and what she'd once thought was cute now looked like a good handle to grab and smash his face into something. Something hard, preferably.

"No, about your chakras… and your attitude. It's really bringing a cloud to the studio," Horatio said and to Paige's shock, he reached out and patted her arm. "I think you need to get some help. I've done what I can, but there's only so much you can work out during yoga. It might be best for you to find a counselor."

"I...what? You're saying this is *my* fault?" Paige's mouth gaped as she pointed from Horatio to the bed.

"There is no blame here," Horatio said, using his soothing yoga voice as though he was trying to calm an unruly dog.

"Yes, Horatio, there *is* blame here. On you, specifically, for cheating on me," Paige enunciated clearly, her body almost vibrating with anger.

"How can there be cheating? I don't cheat. I've always had an open-door policy," Horatio said, shrugging a shoulder and once more reaching out to run a hand down her arm. Paige pulled away from his touch, her mind scrambling as she tried to take in his words.

"Open-door policy to your teachings. To your classes. To your home for rituals or meditation sessions," Paige clarified.

"Yes, for that too."

"But not to your bedroom. *Our* bedroom."

"I never said that."

"Wait...are you telling me that all along..." Paige gulped a breath as her mind flashed back over the past two years. The other students eying her. The whispers. She'd always thought it was because they were envious of her relationship with Horatio. He was a charming man and he'd gathered admirers with ease. Paige had never begrudged any of his students for looking up to him.

"Paige, my goddess, you know I don't believe we're meant to be monogamous."

"I do?" Paige asked, incredulous. She most certainly did *not.*

"Of course. It's too restricting for our carnal nature. We're meant to come together with others, to enjoy the beauty and union that can come from sharing in physical pleasure together. It's important to our chakras that we remain open and welcoming to all."

"I'm fairly certain our chakras can be healthy without my bed being a revolving door of partners."

"That's coming from a place of judgment, Paige. What did I say about that?"

"Judgment comes from fear," Paige said automatically and then clamped her mouth shut. How easily was this man leading her to his side in this argument? What a fool she'd been.

"Exactly. And we shouldn't judge others on their path. This is my path, Paige. I'm meant to share my love and my expertise with the world. It's what I'm here to do. Don't you see? That's why I'm so at peace with myself." Horatio smiled blissfully up at her, assuming Paige would understand.

"I suspect it's the multiple orgasms that have brought you calm, not some higher calling," Paige bit out.

Horatio recoiled as if slapped. "This is what I mean, Paige. Your attitude…well, it needs adjusting. I've tried, but I think it's best if you seek your help elsewhere. I've done all I can here."

"I'm sorry, what? You're…breaking up with *me*? Even though you are the cheater? And the liar?"

"I never cheated or lied. I've always been honest about having an open-door policy."

"A little clarification on what that meant might have been nice before I moved my entire world into yours!" Paige shouted, hands on her hips, fury raging through her. No way was he going to deny her the righteous indignation she was due.

"I don't think I could have been any clearer. Open-door is pretty self-explanatory."

Paige's mouth fell open as she struggled for words. Had she been that blind? Was he in the right about this? Or was he just twisting it for his own benefit? Confusion raced through her as she stared down at him.

"You've a good soul, my goddess, but you need more help with clearing your chakras than I can give. It's time for you to move on. Your path will be lighter for it." Horatio nodded as though he was giving her a roadmap to happiness. He was so sold on his own guru status that he couldn't see he was being a condescending prick. Luckily, Paige wasn't so far gone that she couldn't.

"You're a fake," Paige said, and a storm cloud washed over Horatio's face. "A *fake*. A liar. A user. A manipulator. And you'll never get what you want, no matter how much you seek your path, Horatio. I've never seen dirtier chakras in my life."

Not that Paige could see chakras, but she enjoyed the anger that roiled across Horatio's face.

"It's time for you to pack your things and go," Horatio said.

"Oh, trust me, I was on my way."

"Most of your stuff is packed for the retreat anyway. It shouldn't take long. I'm going for a swim in the meantime." Horatio stood, his tall lanky body hovering over hers before he bent to press a kiss to her head. "Be well, my goddess."

Continue reading today!

The Isle of Destiny Series

ALSO BY TRICIA O'MALLEY

Stone Song

Sword Song

Spear Song

Sphere Song

A completed series.

Available in audio, e-book & paperback!

"Love this series. I will read this multiple times. Keeps you on the edge of your seat. It has action, excitement and romance all in one series."

- Amazon Review

The Wildsong Series

ALSO BY TRICIA O'MALLEY

Song of the Fae

Melody of Flame

Chorus of Ashes

"The magic of Fae is so believable. I read these books in one sitting and can't wait for the next one. These are books you will reread many times."

- Amazon Review

Available in audio, e-book & paperback!

Available Now

The Siren Island Series

ALSO BY TRICIA O'MALLEY

Good Girl

Up to No Good

A Good Chance

Good Moon Rising

Too Good to Be True

A Good Soul

In Good Time

A completed series.

Available in audio, e-book & paperback!

"Love her books and was excited for a totally new and different one! Once again, she did NOT disappoint! Magical in multiple ways and on multiple levels. Her writing style, while similar to that of Nora Roberts, kicks it up a notch!! I want to visit that island, stay in the B&B and meet the gals who run it! The characters are THAT real!!!" - Amazon Review

The Althea Rose Series

ALSO BY TRICIA O'MALLEY

One Tequila

Tequila for Two

Tequila Will Kill Ya (Novella)

Three Tequilas

Tequila Shots & Valentine Knots (Novella)

Tequila Four

A Fifth of Tequila

A Sixer of Tequila

Seven Deadly Tequilas

Eight Ways to Tequila

Tequila for Christmas (Novella)

"Not my usual genre but couldn't resist the Florida Keys setting. I was hooked from the first page. A fun read with just the right amount of crazy! Will definitely follow this series."- Amazon Review

A completed series.

Available in audio, e-book & paperback!

The Mystic Cove Series

Wild Irish Heart

Wild Irish Eyes

Wild Irish Soul

Wild Irish Rebel

Wild Irish Roots: Margaret & Sean

Wild Irish Witch

Wild Irish Grace

Wild Irish Dreamer

Wild Irish Christmas (Novella)

Wild Irish Sage

Wild Irish Renegade

Wild Irish Moon

"I have read thousands of books and a fair percentage have been romances. Until I read Wild Irish Heart, I never had a book actually make me believe in love."- Amazon Review

A completed series.

Available in audio, e-book & paperback!

Also by Tricia O'Malley

STAND ALONE NOVELS

Ms. Bitch

"Ms. Bitch is sunshine in a book! An uplifting story of fighting your way through heartbreak and making your own version of happily-ever-after."

~Ann Charles, USA Today Bestselling Author

Starting Over Scottish

Grumpy. Meet Sunshine.

She's American. He's Scottish. She's looking for a fresh start. He's returning to rediscover his roots.

One Way Ticket

A funny and captivating beach read where booking a one-way ticket to paradise means starting over, letting go, and taking a chance on love…one more time

10 out of 10 - The BookLife Prize

Pencraft Book of the year 2021

Contact Me

Love books? What about fun giveaways? Nope? Okay, can I entice you with underwater photos and cute dogs? Let's stay friends, receive my emails by signing up at my website

www.triciaomalley.com

As always, you can reach me at
info@triciaomalley.com

Or find me on Facebook and Instagram.
@triciaomalleyauthor

Author's Acknowledgement

A very deep and heartfelt *thank you* goes to those in my life who have continued to support me on this wonderful journey of being an author. At times, this job can be very stressful, however, I'm grateful to have the sounding board of my friends who help me through the trickier moments of self-doubt. An extra-special thanks goes to The Scotsman, who is my number one supporter and always manages to make me smile.

Please know that every book I write is a part of me, and I hope you feel the love that I put into my stories. Without my readers, my work means nothing, and I am grateful that you all are willing to share your valuable time with the worlds I create. I hope each book brings a smile to your face and for just a moment it gives you a much-needed escape.

Slainté,
Tricia O'Malley

Made in the USA
Columbia, SC
23 April 2023

15727891R00140